Gods, Monsters, and
the Lucky Peach

GODS, MONSTERS, AND THE LUCKY PEACH

KELLY ROBSON

A TOM DOHERTY ASSOCIATES BOOK

NEW YORK

This is a work of fiction. All of the characters, organizations, and events portrayed in this novella are either products of the author's imagination or are used fictitiously.

GODS, MONSTERS, AND THE LUCKY PEACH

Cover illustration by Jon Foster
Cover design by Christine Foltzer

Edited by Ellen Datlow

A Tor.com Book
Published by Tom Doherty Associates
175 Fifth Avenue
New York, NY 10010

www.tor.com

Tor® is a registered trademark of
Macmillan Publishing Group, LLC.

ISBN 978-1-250-16384-4 (ebook)
ISBN 978-1-250-16385-1 (trade paperback)

First Edition: March 2018

For Alyx, always

The past is another country;
we want to colonize it.

Gods, Monsters, and
the Lucky Peach

1

THE MONSTER LOOKED LIKE an old grandmother from the waist up, but it had six long octopus legs. It crawled out of its broken egg and cowered in the muddy drainage ditch. When it noticed Shulgi, its jaw fell open, exposing teeth too perfect to be human.

It recoiled and hissed: *Oh-shit-shit-shit-shit-shit-shit.*

Shulgi hefted his flail in one hand and his scythe in the other. He knew his duty better than anyone other than the gods. Kings were made for killing monsters.

~

On one of Calgary's wide, south-facing orchard terraces, Minh pruned peach trees while paying vague attention to ESSA's weekly business meeting. Minh and her partners were all plague babies. They'd worked together for nearly sixty years, so unless a problem cropped up—an over-budget project or a scope-creeping client—their fakes could handle the meeting nearly unmonitored.

No problems this week. Nobody playing diva, simply

letting their fakes walk through the agenda. Everyone except for Kiki, the firm's ridiculously frenetic young admin. She was playing with an antique paper clip simulation, stringing them into ropes. The clips clicked against the table.

Kiki, stop it, Minh whispered. *The sound is driving me nuts.*

I didn't know you were lurking, Kiki replied. *I thought I was all alone here.*

The meetings are important. Sit still and listen.

Easy for you to say. You don't spend every Monday morning with a bunch of fakes. I bet you're halfway up a tree right now, aren't you?

Minh didn't reply. She was in a tree—four legs wrapped around the trunk of Calgary's oldest peach. She'd just started the late-winter pruning. Below her, bots gathered the dropped limbs and piled them on a cargo float. A cold downwash funneled through the orchard, the wind caught and guided by the hab's towering south wall. Minh pinged the microclimate sensors. A few more weeks of winter chill and the trees could start moving into bud break.

Since I've got your attention, Kiki continued, *you might want to look over the RFP coming up next. It's a big river remediation project funded by a private bank. You've never seen anything like it. You're going to disintegrate.*

Kiki shot her the request for proposal package with a flick of her fingernail.

Minh dropped out of the tree and spread the data over the orchard's carefully manicured ground cover. She hadn't seen a new project in ten years. The banks weren't interested. Calgary and all the other surface habitats struggled to keep their ongoing projects alive. Some of the habs—Edmonton, notoriously—had managed the funding crisis so badly, they'd starved themselves out.

Before she'd even finished scanning the introductory material, Minh's blood pressure was spiraling.

A time travel project. Aren't you excited? Kiki whispered. *I nearly blew apart when I saw it.*

Half the RFP made sense. Past state assessment, flow modeling, ecological remediation—her life's work, familiar as her own skin. The rest didn't make sense at all. Mesopotamia, Tigris, Euphrates—words out of history. And time travel—those two words raised the hairs on the back of her neck. Her biom flashed with blood pressure alerts.

It's intriguing, whispered Minh. *Why didn't you send it to me earlier?*

Kiki jangled the paper clips. *It's been in your queue for two days. I've been bugging your fake about it. You never look at your RFPs before the meeting. None of you do.*

Yeah, well, we're busy people, Minh replied absently.

When the plague babies had moved to the surface six decades earlier, in 2205, they'd been determined to prove humanity could escape the hives and hells and live above ground again, in humanity's ancestral habitat. First, they'd erected bare-bones habs high in the mountains, scraping together skeleton funding for proof-of-concept pilot projects. For the first few ecological remediation projects, the plague babies donated their billable hours, hoping to lure investment and spark population growth.

It worked. Not quite as quickly as they'd hoped, but over the decades, the habs proved viable. Iceland and Cusco were booming. Calgary wasn't quite as successful but momentum was building. Then TERN developed time travel, and every aboveground initiative had stalled.

Why would TERN get involved in river remediation now? Hadn't they ruined her life enough already?

Minh's biom slid an alert into the middle of her eye. Blood pressure wildly fluctuating, as if Minh couldn't tell. She'd been light-headed ever since opening the RFP package. Her field of vision was narrowing. Her fingers itched to dial a little relief into her biom, but no. Minh had promised her medtech she wouldn't meddle with her hormonal balance, so instead of hitting herself with a jolt of adrenaline, she circled the peach tree's central leader with two legs and hung upside down, rough bark against her back, and let the blood cascade to her brain.

Back in the meeting, the fakes finished walking through the project progress reports. Nothing over budget. No problems. The fakes approved them all.

"Okay," Kiki told the fakes. "On to new opportunities."

Watch this, she whispered to Minh. *I can turn these fakes into scientists.*

Kiki fired the time travel RFP onto the table.

"The first one is for Minh. River remediation, and it's big. Thousands of billable hours."

All round the table, the fakes dropped away as Minh's partners engaged with the text.

Kiki grinned at Minh. *See? It's like magic.*

Mesopotamian Development Bank Request for Proposal (RFP 2267-16)
Past State Assessment of the Mesopotamian Trench

Due March 21, 2267 at 14:00 GMT

The Mesopotamian Development Bank is embarking on a multiphase initiative to remediate the Mesopotamian trench. This project will restore 100,000 square kilometers of habitat, including the natural channels of the Euphrates and Tigris rivers, their tributaries, coastal wetlands, and terrestrial and aquatic species. The restoration project will support a network of arcologies across the habitat.

The Bank is seeking a multidisciplinary project team to execute a past state assessment supported by the Temporal Economic Research Node (TERN), a division of the Centers for Excellence in Economic Research and Development (CEERD). The successful proponent team will assess and quantify the environmental state of Mesopotamia in 2024 BCE. The project will include complete geomorphological and ecological baselines, responses to stressors, and processes of change and adaptation. The data gathered will guide and inform future restoration projects in an effort to impose a regular climatic regime across the Mesopotamian drainage basin.

"This project is too good to pass up," said Minh. "I want it."

"You can't be serious, Minh," David said. He was out of breath, puffing hard. "Nobody hates CEERD and TERN more than you."

Minh pinged his location. David was cycling the Icefields Guideway, climbing Sunwapta Pass without boost assist.

"It's a great job," said Minh. "I've already started working on the proposal."

Kiki rolled her eyes. Minh ignored her.

"This isn't a job, it's a joke," said Sarah. "You can't do an ecological assessment on a hundred thousand square kilometers in three weeks. Three years wouldn't be enough."

Zhang shook his head. "Maybe if we knew this bank, but we've never even heard of them."

Kiki fired a documentary onto the table. "The Mesopotamian Development Bank specializes in West Asian projects. They're designing a string of habs for the Zagros Mountains. Look at this design. You're going to collapse."

The table exploded into a full-blown architectural simulation, the angles and planes of a huge ziggurat echoing the peaks and crags of the surrounding ranges. In comparison, Calgary was a pimple on the prairie.

"Put the doc away, Kiki," said Sarah. "It's just pretty pictures to attract investment."

Kiki slapped the doc down. Minh threw some numbers into an opportunity-assessment matrix and fired it onto the table.

"If we win, the follow-on work could be massive," she said. "Make the client happy and they'll keep us fed for decades."

Minh's partners reviewed the figures in the follow-on column.

"I like the numbers," said Clint. "But the job's got to be wired."

Kiki leaned over the table, braids swinging. "If they already know who they want to hire, why bother with a public procurement process? Private banks don't need procurement transparency."

Easy, Minh whispered. *I'm handling this.*

"I want this job," said Minh. "I've already started putting together my team."

David said, "If you win, your team can't pull out. The Bank of Calgary would peel the skin off us."

"It won't be a problem," said Minh. "Who wouldn't jump at the chance to time travel?"

2

WHEN THE NEW STARS appeared, Shulgi was in the arms of his new wife, a soft, fragrant widow who spoke with an endearing lisp. Still young, she'd already brought two healthy children into the world with ease. She was a proud and capable mother, and when she'd promised him more children than any of his other wives, Shulgi laughed.

It was his last moment of joy.

~

The next day, Kiki showed up at Minh's door.

She was huge. More than half a meter taller than Minh, Kiki outweighed her by at least sixty kilos. Like all fat babies, she was flawless. Perfectly proportioned and so healthy, her flesh seemed to burst with the pent-up energy of youth.

She wore an all-weather coverall and lugged a backpack. Her brown face was pearled with sweat, and her pedal clips scraped over the catwalk grid as she shifted the heavy pack from one shoulder to the other.

"Hi," Kiki said. "Sorry to surprise you. I told your fake I was coming, but I guess you haven't checked your queue yet."

Kiki belonged to one of the half-assed hybrid habs the fat babies were building up north. Minh couldn't remember which one. She pinged Kiki's ID. Jasper, right.

Minh blinked up at her. "Did you bike all the way here in one day?"

She'd never given Kiki much thought, aside from the occasional administrative tangle. But here she was, large as life. One of Minh's neighbors, a sanitation engineer with cat's-paw prostheses, tried to edge by on the atrium catwalk. Kiki's backpack was in the way. She shrugged it off and hugged the wall to let them pass.

"I left at dawn," said Kiki. "I wanted to take the scenic route, but Jasper doesn't have rights to use the Icefields Guideway. I had to go through Edmonton. Haven't been back there in five years—not since I got out of the crèche. It's falling to pieces. A ghost town."

It was rude to keep Kiki standing outside, but showing up at her studio uninvited was rude too. Minh crossed her arms and leaned against the doorjamb.

"What are you doing in Calgary?" she asked.

Kiki grinned. Even her teeth were big.

"David's giving me full-time hours to help you with

the time travel proposal. If we're going to work together on a big job, I need to able to talk to you. Your fake hates me."

Minh drew herself up a bit taller. No use. If she wanted to talk to Kiki eye-to-eye instead of staring at her sternum, she'd have to climb the doorframe.

"I don't need help. You shouldn't have come all this way."

"Your fake said the same thing. You haven't changed your mind, have you? You seemed excited in the meeting. Excited for you, I mean. You don't exactly emote."

Minh had been ignoring her project deadlines to do preliminary research on West Asia. A literature search on the Tigris and Euphrates left her with a shortlist of several thousand papers, all three hundred years old, but no problem. She knew how to decipher old academic English. The time travel aspect was another matter entirely. No information available at all. If anyone had ever done an ecological assessment using time travel, they weren't talking about it. TERN's nondisclosure agreement had fangs. Big ones.

Minh tried to keep her expression as bland as a fake.

"No, I haven't changed my mind. I'm working on the proposal."

"Then you need help. I checked your utilization projections. You have three report deadlines over the next two weeks. You're in the middle of pruning the orchard on Crowchild Terrace. Plus, you must get pulled into lots of maintenance work. Calgary is an old hab. Falling apart."

"You don't know what you're talking about." Minh hooked a leg on the wall and drew herself taller. "Calgary is doing just fine."

Kiki's face fell. "Sorry."

"I don't have to work in the peach orchard. I do it because I like it. I planted the first trees myself."

Kiki winced. "Come on, Minh. I dropped all my other jobs to work on this. If David throws me back to quarter time, Jasper will be in deep trouble. We traded my extra hours for an advanced civil engineering seminar from U-Bang. Half the hab has already started the course. Maybe you don't need me, but it can't hurt. Give me a chance."

Minh bit back a retort. If the fat babies had stayed in Calgary instead of running off to start their own habs, they'd be fine. Or if they had to leave, at the very least, they could build aboveground using Calgary's hab tech, which was time-tested and proven. Racking up a trade deficit with the Bank of Calgary was better than taking handouts from Bangladesh Hell.

But the young had to go their own way. Minh had to admit she'd been the same, back in the dim and distant past.

Remembering her youth didn't make dealing with fat babies any easier. Minh found young people exhausting. Five years' teaching at the University of Tuktoyaktuk hadn't helped. When Tuk-U shut down, giving up face-to-face teaching was almost a relief.

Minh had been heartbroken, though. Tuktoyaktuk was a jewel box of a hab. The crowning glory of the Arctic, on the wide, fertile Mackenzie River delta, the hab represented the dreams she'd worked toward all her life. But Tuktoyaktuk had failed. Calgary couldn't support it. The bankers hadn't been clever enough. After the university shut down, Minh had tried to block the Bank of Calgary from leasing the hab to CEERD, but she'd lost that fight too.

Losing Tuktoyaktuk still hurt. For Minh, the time travel project was an opportunity to poke CEERD in the eye—not only for Tuktoyaktuk but also for creating TERN and inventing time travel in the first place. If they hadn't, life on the surface of the planet would be different. The banks would still be interested in the investment opportunities the habs offered, and the populations of the hells would be looking to the future instead of the past.

If only she could figure out a way to win the project. Minh couldn't deny her proposal would have to be unusually clever. Winning depended on finding the right strategy, which would take a lot of research. Minh couldn't work twenty-hour days, not anymore. A lifetime of abuse had nearly ruined her health. She needed to find a thin edge and wedge it hard. Kiki might be that edge.

"Fine. You can help. But you can't stay here. I don't have room."

Kiki peered over Minh's head into the studio. Her eyes went wide.

"Wow. Your space is tiny. I bet you can sit on your sofa and reach everything with your tentacles."

"They're called legs."

"Sorry. Legs. You're a firm partner, a senior consultant. You helped build Calgary. But your home is barely bigger than a sleep stack." Kiki's voice rose, incredulous.

"Ecologists don't impress the bankers. You should know that by now."

"So, are we working, or what?"

Minh stood aside and let Kiki into the studio. She loved her home, especially the ten square meters of window looking west at the front ranges of the Rockies, but with Kiki inside, it suddenly felt small.

I'm getting old, Minh thought. *Set in my ways.* Kiki was just an average young human, energetic and disgustingly healthy. A few weeks working together wouldn't do Minh any harm. And a little youthful enthusiasm wouldn't hurt the proposal at all.

3

LOUNGING IN THE COMFORT and luxury of the palace's inner courtyards, enjoying the company of his wives and children, Shulgi might have been the last to notice the new stars if one of his falconers hadn't sent word.

New stars were powerful portents, but their interpretation depended on the skill of the seer and the clarity of their conversations with the gods. Anyone could pretend to read an augury; anyone could say the gods talked to them. But gods rarely spoke plainly. For Shulgi, the gods' voices were usually only echoes of his own desires.

Shulgi only truly trusted one priest: Susa, who spoke for the moon.

~

Minh put Kiki to work researching time travel, tasking her with prying up details about TERN and their technology. It wouldn't be easy. CEERD moved mountains to keep their think tanks' intellectual property classified as trade secrets. Even when the World Economic Commission ruled entire sectors of their work public domain, they shared as little as possible. Those lawsuits ate millions of billable hours.

Minh thought Kiki wouldn't last long working out of her little studio, but it was fine. Kiki left whenever she got restless, and Minh was in and out too. But on the second evening, Minh came home late from a friend's centenary to find Kiki on her sofa. She hadn't bothered to slide it into sleep config. When Minh nudged her elbow with a toe, Kiki didn't even move.

Minh borrowed a hammock from her neighbor and slung it in front of her window. Kiki slept through the whole noisy operation.

The next morning, Minh woke with her nose grazing the glass, drinking in a two-hundred-degree panorama of bright late-winter morning, brown hills in the distance and blue sky above framing the high front ranges of the Rockies, the half-frozen Bow River snaking toward Calgary. A familiar view, but its beauty could still put a crack in her heart.

Minh stayed in the hammock all morning, throwing the West Asian climate data into a key-value database, then painting the mountains with data, using the view for a playground as she ingested enough data to fake an expertise in the ecology and geology of West Asia.

Kiki's feet bumped the wall as she stretched out on the sofa.

"Sorry." Kiki gathered up her clothes and began stuffing them into her backpack. "I couldn't get a sleep stack. Tonight, I'll find a lolly and double up."

Kiki kept her head down, braids veiling her expression.

Why would Kiki insist on staying in Calgary? Jasper must be full of friends, lovers, crèche-mates. Once the proposal was submitted, Kiki would drop back to quarter time. It could take months to replace the billable hours she'd dropped to work with Minh.

But if she wanted to be in Calgary, it must be important. The reasons were none of Minh's business.

"It's okay," Minh said. "You can have the sofa."

"Really?" Kiki's grin shone brighter than the sun coming through the windows. She trotted into the bathroom. Her voice echoed off the tiles. "Thanks, Minh. I don't like to fuck strangers, actually. Or anyone, really. I don't get much out of it."

Minh's eyebrows rose. Maybe that was why Kiki was in Calgary. Taking a break from the hormonal atmosphere at home.

"That must be hard in Jasper. You'd be odd person out."

"Yeah, Jasper's pretty sticky."

Kelly Robson

"So, what do you do? Dial up the oxytocin and join the crowd, or hibernate and avoid it?"

Kiki stuck her head out of the bathroom. The beads on her braids clicked against the doorjamb.

"Don't you know? Jasper doesn't offer full biom control. We can't float the license fees."

Minh gritted her teeth. "Oh, right. I forgot."

Personal autonomy was a central tenet of the above-ground movement. When the plague babies ascended from the hells, they'd spent years in clinics and hospitals, poked and prodded by surgeons and physical therapists. Escaping that life was one of the reasons they'd moved to the surface in the first place. The habs offered their people complete power over their own bodies. Minh had managed her own health since she was twenty.

Trust the fat babies to throw that freedom away.

"I tried joining in the sex games a couple of times, but I don't see the point. I'd rather spend my time doing useful work, you know?"

Minh nodded. "Doing important work is all that matters."

Kiki grinned. "No wonder you and I get along so well." She disappeared into the bathroom again.

"Do we?" Minh muttered, scowling.

Maybe they did. Kiki approached time travel research with energy and determination, quickly accumulating a pile of annotated bookmarks for a solid and substantial literature search report. Minh was making progress too, soaking up old West Asian ecological research papers.

She was itching to dive into a work plan draft, but her project deadlines loomed. Mesopotamia would have to wait. Minh put the research aside and tried to drum up enthusiasm for yet another Icelandic adaptive management review. But that evening, Calgary's water recirculation system blew. All available residents were pulled into the refit. Minh spent an eighteen-hour shift crawling up and down pipe shafts, troubleshooting the repair bots.

When Minh dragged herself home from her first shift, Kiki was waiting.

"I'm still researching time travel," Kiki said. "If you want, I can pull work plans from old proposals so you don't have to face a blank page when the refit is done. Just point me in the right direction."

Minh peeled off her wet coverall. "Dig out the proposal for the Colorado River current-state assessment. The target area is about the same size."

"Which bank is remediating the Colorado River?"

Minh shut herself in the bathroom and threw her clothes in the sink.

None of them, she whispered. *They yanked the funding ten years ago. Make a list of all the data-gathering tech we used in Colorado. Satellites, cameras, sampling, and so on.*

We'll have to take all the infrastructure back in time with us.

You'll be launching satellites?

Of course. I'm not going to measure river flow with a handheld doppler.

No water in the shower, not until the refit was done. Minh slathered herself with cleanser and toweled herself dry. Then she gripped the shower walls with her three right legs and hung upside down. She loosened her left legs and slid open the shield protecting the teratoma on her lower hip. After cleaning it thoroughly, she slathered the prosthesis socket with lubricant gel. Then she repeated the process on her right side. When she was done, she hung from the wall and let her arms hang, stretching the kinks out of her back and shoulders.

Careful curation of her glucose and blood oxygen levels had kept her alert through the whole long shift, but now she needed rest. Her body thrummed with exhaustion.

If she couldn't fall asleep naturally, she'd ping her medtech. In the past, she would have tweaked herself asleep. No more, though. She'd done enough damage. Standard hormonal protocols only from now on.

Which gave Minh the glimmer of an idea.

She wrapped herself in a soft jumper and opened the bathroom door.

"TERN must have a standard project protocol. They

take tourists to the past. No way they do it without power and tech."

Kiki nodded. "The only official information is from the marketing for TERN's package tours. They claim ambient power is fully available in the past. I've tried to get more specifics, but I get canned replies saying TERN's intellectual property rights are ratified by the World Economic Commission."

Minh snorted. "CEERD and all its rotten think tanks believe if they game the system enough, the World Economic Commission will turn them all into private banks and then they can roll around in their credit."

Kiki laughed. "You really hate them."

"They're greedy. But maybe we can make it work for us." Minh hooked a leg on the hammock and hauled herself up. "What have you found out about the client?"

Kiki sat cross-legged on the sofa, in a nest of quilts.

"The Mesopotamian Development Bank was created last year. Their identity isn't public yet, so all I have are rumors. They might be a mechanical engineer from one of the Siberian hives who developed a way to tunnel through burning peat, or a neurosurgical engineer from Bangladesh who found a new way to splice neurons."

"The World Economic Commission loves engineers."

Minh dimmed the lights and closed her eyes. Maintenance bots danced in patterns behind her eyelids. She'd never get to sleep.

"The client only just became a private bank, but they're already investigating a massive project. That's quick," Minh said.

"I guess they like Mesopotamia a lot."

"So it's a passion project."

Minh squirmed, trying to get comfortable. She slipped one leg out of the hammock and pushed against the window, rocking herself back and forth. Maybe it would help her get to sleep. She hated bothering her tech.

"A passion project," Minh repeated. "Which means . . ." Her biom nagged her, flashing unusually strident cortisol alerts and demanding rest. "I'm too tired to figure it out. Remind me about it tomorrow."

"Okay. And what about the project team?"

Minh hadn't even thought about team members yet.

"I'm working on it," she said.

4

SHULGI TRUSTED SUSA BECAUSE she never told him what he wanted to hear. She didn't care for his good opinion and never made any effort to gain his favor. In fact, she hated him. The moment she got within ten steps of him, her nose would wrinkle up as though he smelled foul. It made no difference whether he were stewing in training-pit sweat or fresh and oiled from a bath. Shulgi never smelled sweet to her.

When Shulgi had become king, Susa ascended the dais of the moon. Her duty was to oppose him. As woman opposes man, as humans strain against the gods, as children defy their parents, Susa's right and duty was to say yes when he said no and argue against his every decision.

But she didn't have to take such pleasure in it.

~

By the time Calgary's refit was done, the Bank of Calgary was nagging Minh for a draft budget. The submission deadline was only a few days away, and Minh still hadn't done anything about her project team.

Ten years back, when news of the first time travel project hit, she'd been wrapping up the Colorado River current-state assessment. Her entire thirty-person multidisciplinary team camped on the edge of the Grand Canyon, accompanied by a professional media crew and a dozen cameras, exploiting the canyon's spectacular visuals as they trapped the documentary data for the final report. It was a waste of billable hours, but banks liked grand gestures and mediagenic visuals. The funding had been available back then.

The Colorado River was envisioned as the largest riverine restoration project ever undertaken, extending from La Poudre Pass to the gulf, supporting a string of habs—eight glistening green pearls along the great river from mountains to sea, providing habitat for a hundred million people within four centuries.

Minh had been skeptical. But there was no reason they couldn't remediate the first few reaches, support a few new habs. Even one would benefit the funding consortium eventually. She had planned to plant the first glacier seed herself. Maybe she would have even seen a little streamflow before she died.

Then the time travel news hit and all work stopped.

At first, the whole Colorado team was transfixed

by the news docs. When they began arguing over the implications of time travel, some predicted disaster—temporal disturbances and out-of-control paradoxes. Most were enchanted by the possibility of restoring extinct species—rewilding on a scale they'd never dreamed of. Personally, Minh was excited by the idea of time-traveling adaptive management projects. She could initiate a restoration initiative, visit the future to see the results, then come back to the present day and fine-tune the approach. But her excitement was short-lived; time travel could only be used to visit the past.

Not even Minh foresaw what actually happened: the banks lost interest in everything aboveground, and especially in long-term ecological restoration projects.

People—especially bankers—had trouble thinking long-term, and nothing was more long-term than ecological restoration. Results took decades, even with soil printers, glacier seeds, climatic baffles, wind chutes—all the tech they'd developed. Even when harnessing the wind-sculpting and rain-generating power of the great mountain ranges of the globe, restoring natural habitats took vision, determination, and, most importantly, glacial patience.

Banks were not patient. When they saw a shortcut, they lunged for it. No matter if the shortcut was an illusion. No matter that time travel couldn't be used to change anything.

The funding pool dried up. Ambitious new restoration projects died in the planning phase, never to be resurrected. The habs formed desperate consortiums to keep their projects afloat, fees plunged in all related disciplines, and the few surviving projects operated on shallow budgets with skeleton teams.

After a long, dry decade, interest in ecological restoration was starting to trickle back, but the damage was done. The Colorado River would stay dry. Probably forever.

Kiki passed a mug of tea up to Minh as she lay in her hammock. She'd slept ten hours straight. Probably snoring openmouthed the whole time, judging by her throbbing headache.

"I'm looking through TERN's earliest docs," said Kiki. "Why were they so concerned with proving time travel can't affect anything? Wasn't it obvious? Time travel happened. Nothing changed."

Minh swished the tea around her parched mouth and swallowed.

"No, it wasn't obvious at all. You were still in the crèche, right? How old?"

"Thirteen."

"Easy to take things on faith at that age. I was seventy-three. TERN wouldn't share their research. No open peer review process, no repeatable results. Plus, their public relations department was releasing disinformation to keep critics confused. Everyone I knew was suspicious. How could we trust them not to mess with history?"

"TERN says that when they time travel, a separate timeline is spun off from ours, and when the time travelers leave, the timeline collapses."

Minh shrugged. "TERN can say anything they want. They have a monopoly. Nobody can prove them wrong, because nobody outside TERN knows how it works."

"Have you seen this?"

Kiki shot a doc into the middle of the room. The Pyramid of the Sun at Teotihuacan bloomed across the floor and stretched up to the ceiling.

Minh winced. Her headache pounded. She shot the doc out the window. The pyramid grew to full size over the river valley.

Sunlight bounced off the back of Minh's skull. She lifted a leg to her forehead and squeezed her temples. Her biom blinked a low-priority dehydration alert.

A hundred puffs of dust pocked the surface of the pyramid. The stones shuddered and slipped, then the whole huge structure disappeared behind a cloud of dust. When it cleared, the pyramid lay like a corpse, a pile of cold rubble across the Avenue of the Dead.

The doc overlaid the rubble with a dozen time-stamped satellite images of the pyramid in real time, here and now, whole and undamaged. Kiki killed the doc.

"Yeah, I've seen it." Minh clambered out of the hammock and grabbed a bottle of water. "When TERN finally proved time travel was effectively useless, I figured everything would go back to normal and the banks would get interested in us again. I was wrong."

"That's why you hate CEERD and TERN."

"One of the reasons." Minh drained the water bottle and wiped her lips with the back of her hand. "What have you found out about the project's restrictive parameters?"

"Payload," Kiki said. "That's the big one."

Kiki took her through a stack of bookmarks. She'd analyzed hundreds of time travel docs, estimating the mass and volume of the cast, crew, and equipment. Her analysis was confirmed by a stack of other calculations, including the capacity of time travel tourist groups, and details of all known artifacts retrieved from the past.

Kiki sat cross-legged on the sofa, pulled her braids back, and knotted them at the nape of her neck.

"TERN's maximum payload seems to be restricted by volume, not mass. The single heaviest item brought from the past is the Golden Buddha from ancient Thailand. It weighs over five thousand kilograms."

Minh flipped through the bookmarks and scanned the attached notes. Kiki's analysis was solid, her conclusions well supported. Impressive.

"You should publish these results," she said.

Kiki grinned. "I can't. It's TERN's intellectual property."

Then she whispered, *I bet I'm not the first person to figure this out. Every time someone tries to publish results like this, using open and available information, TERN shuts them down. I've been whispering with a plague baby in Sudbury Hell who hates TERN even more than you do.*

Okay, I get it. No more bad-mouthing TERN if we want to win this work.

Minh plucked at her temples with her suckers. The headache was easing off. Time to get to work.

Minh used Kiki's numbers to mock up the payload dimensions. The volume amounted to a little more than half her studio.

"This can't be right. There's no room for equipment."

"There is, actually. Almost everything can be fabbed." Kiki shot an array of color-coded rectangles into the mock-up, stacking them like crèche blocks. A large yellow cube flashed. "That's the fab, and the layer on the bottom is super-dense feedstock. You can even bring a skip along for transportation. All you need are the skip drives, sensory array, and safety-foam canisters." A dozen shoe-sized pink boxes stacked on top of the yellow cube. "If you want to bring lots of satellites, it's easy. They're small. You can take plenty."

Minh paced the edges of the mock-up, thinking.

"People take up a lot of space. They can't be compressed."

Minh added blocks to represent monitoring and sampling equipment. She threw in a few placeholders for the team's personal effects, water treatment system, and a nutritional extruder. A third of the payload was still empty.

Minh's aches and pains faded into the background, overwhelmed by the electric thrill jolting from fingers to the tips of her legs.

"I got it," Minh shouted. Kiki jumped, startled.

Minh lowered her voice to a reasonable level. "This is how I'll win the project."

"You're sure?" Kiki asked. "You sound pretty sure."

Minh laughed. "No, but it's not impossible."

Kiki beamed. "How?"

"The client is asking for a multidisciplinary team. That's old lingo, from the big-budget days. Our competitors will stack their proposals with consultants—everything from fisheries biologists to fluvial engineers to statisticians. Big teams, lots of billable hours, like the old days."

"And our team—your team, I mean?"

"My team will be small." Minh grinned. "The smallest."

-5-

WHEN SUSA SENT FOR Shulgi, he gathered his household and processed through the streets, accompanied by everyone who belonged to him, from his eldest wife to the child who swept the stairs. Susa and her people met them at the apex of the ziggurat. She looked agitated, tired, unwell, her skin sallow under the layer of cosmetic.

She tried to rush through their greeting ritual, as if she didn't have time to honor the gods, but Shulgi wouldn't allow himself to be hurried. With new stars watching, he told her, they mustn't scatter the grain of duty for others to glean.

The delay made Susa furious. When the ritual was complete, she spoke plainly.

The stars were the clearest augury she'd ever seen and could only be interpreted one way. The stars called for Shulgi's death.

∼

Hamid's fake was dressed in cowboy gear. It looked like a refugee from a crèche costume party.

"I'm busy, Minh," it said. "Tell me what you want."

Minh ground her teeth in frustration. "I need to talk to Hamid."

Thousands of billable hours, Kiki whispered. *Those are the magic words.*

Hamid doesn't care. His lover is a private bank.

"What's it about? I'll pass the message on," the fake drawled.

"It's a new project. A unique opportunity. Can you boost me up his queue? Top priority."

The fake nodded and faded out.

"Wait," Minh said. The fake faded back in. She shot it the RFP package. "Tell him to look at this and think about the horses."

"The budget is due in ten minutes," Kiki said. "We need to submit now. No room to wiggle."

Their draft budget had two big blanks. Minh was still the only team member.

"Put Hamid in."

"Without his permission?"

"He's an old friend. And this is a just a draft."

"Okay. I'm putting myself in the other blank."

"Kiki—"

"Do you have a better idea? The bank will like it. Call

me a placeholder. You can kick me off the team anytime you like."

"Okay, it's better than a blank."

"*Better than a blank*. That's my new motto."

Kiki sealed the budget and shot it upstairs.

When the Bank of Calgary called two hours later, they were both deep into editing—Kiki finessing a custom version of ESSA's history and past projects into an inspiring three minutes, Minh pulling the guts out of the old Colorado work plan and trying to reshape it into a credible approach to a past-state assessment.

Minh should have known the bank would jump fast. Calgary was deep into trade deficit. This RFP was a big ripe peach hanging on the branch. Of course the bank was itching to grab it.

Even so, Minh knew exactly what the bankers would say. It was what they always said.

The banker intercepted Minh and Kiki the moment they walked out of the elevator onto Calgary's bustling apex floor.

"These rates are too low," he said, ushering them into a glass-walled conference room.

He was young—a tall fat baby with bony wrists protruding from the sleeves of his banker suit. She'd seen him before, in the entourage of Calgary's senior account manager. Now he had his own entourage—three more fat babies, big-eyed and downy-faced. Looked like they were right out of the crèche.

"Where's Rosa?" Minh looked around for the banker she usually dealt with, an elegant white-haired plague baby who wheeled around in an antique chair.

"Palliative care. But she still has team oversight."

Minh winced. Rosa was only a few years older than her.

"About these rates—"

Minh cut the banker off. "I don't want to lose this job on price."

"There's no point in proposing a tiny team with cut rates. Your fees will be a minor line item compared to what TERN will be charging the Mesopotamian Development Bank."

"You think the client won't care what we cost? In my experience, private banks are cheap. They only value their own expertise. Everyone else is just a warm body."

"Not this private bank. Their pockets are deep."

"Oh, good." Minh plastered on a phony smile. "You've got intel. Tell me everything."

His eyes glazed over, descending into the data stream.

Minh exchanged a glance with Kiki. *He's whispering with Rosa, I bet. He's not as good as you are at running multiple streams.*

Why are you poking him?

I want him scared of me. He needs to learn I can't be pushed around.

The banker looked up from his stream. "The Mesopotamian Development Bank is private."

"Obviously," said Minh. "Tell me who they are. What do they want?"

"Unknown."

Minh grimaced. All this would be so much easier with Rosa.

"You don't know anything about the client. You have no intel or insight, but you want to tell me how to budget this project."

The banker spread his hands in an awkward version of the conciliatory gesture bankers always made when they were out of their depth. He was trying to seem friendly and understanding, but his expression was wary.

"Our models show ESSA should be contributing more to Calgary's economy. Your firm has been treading water for years. You're a top consultant in two fields, fluvial geomorphology and restoration ecology. Clients should expect to pay well for your time."

Minh gave the banker an icy smile.

Watch this, Kiki. This is how I handle a bully banker.

Minh drew several of her legs up onto the table, held tight, and leaned in. "Let me tell you something." She smacked the glass with her toe and dropped her voice into its lowest register. "I've been running projects for forty years. Out there." She pointed out the window at the mountains. "In the real world, not hiding up here in the top levels of a hab someone else built, juggling numbers and pretending to be important."

He sat back in his chair. A shade of alarm contorted his young face, but then he relaxed.

Rosa's telling him how to handle me.

Minh lifted another leg and pointed at the underside of the glass spire overhead. "When I was your age, I helped build this hab. My team put the capstone into place. I know how to win a job and deliver results."

She gripped the edges of the table with two legs and thrust herself forward, right in the banker's face. "All you do is push deficits around and procrastinate until the hab collapses."

The banker looked ruffled, but Rosa was keeping him under control. "We'll take your budget recommendations into consideration. But one more thing—"

Here it comes. He's going to try to hobble me.

"Calgary doesn't want you to put yourself at risk on a dangerous project. Your maintenance contributions are valuable, especially snowpack management. Certainly, you should be on the team as project advisor, working from Calgary, but not project lead."

Minh pretended to consider it for a moment.

"There's a studio available," the banker continued. "High level, over a hundred square meters."

I bet that's Rosa's space, Minh whispered. *Banker level.*

"Which way does it face?" Minh asked.

"I don't—" The banker glazed over for a half-second. "East. It faces the old city."

Minh tapped a leg against the underside of the glass table, still pretending to consider the offer.

I've never seen you in diva mode before, Minh. You're pretty good at it.

This is nothing. Wait until you meet Hamid.

After letting the banker fidget for a minute, she said, "No, thanks. If you don't want us to bid on this project, we can flush our proposal, right, Kiki?"

"Sure. Iceland wants another adaptive management review. They requested a quote this morning."

The banker huffed and puffed for another ten minutes before winding up the meeting. As they walked to the elevator, he fell into step beside Kiki.

"Glad to see ESSA's finally doing succession planning," he said.

Kiki grinned at Minh, triumphant. *See? I told you the bank would like having me on the team.*

6

THE OTHER PRIESTS BACKED up Susa's interpretation—the stars called for Shulgi's death. Twelve priests, all agreed on an omen, all interpreting a sign the same way? Impossible. They couldn't agree what direction the sun rose from. There was only one explanation: they'd decided upon it previously.

Shulgi knew they'd been arguing, in a terrible hush, for months. He had expected a petition to expand the borders of the kingdom. But no—this must be it. Susa wanted him dead. When the new stars appeared, she forced the omen's interpretation to suit her needs. Dazzled by the force of her will, the other priests fell into line.

~

Minh and Kiki hooked their bikes onto the guideway ramp and cruised west, ducking behind the bikes' plexiform windbreaks and pedaling hard to keep warm in the chill. Ponds of meltwater dotted the shortgrass prairie below.

Kiki lagged behind for a minute, then put on a burst of speed and zoomed past, laughing.

I'm sorry, Minh. I don't want to be mean, but you look really funny.

What? Minh looked down at her prostheses, two legs on each pedal and the remaining two curled around the frame.

An octopus riding a bike.

Minh bore down on the pedals and raced past Kiki, waving two of her legs.

Getting out of Calgary felt wonderful. Breathing the sharp, clean mountain air, letting Calgary's stepped ziggurat shrink in the distance, leaving behind the dry eastern wasteland where the old city lay under dust, a reminder that similar devastation lay beyond every horizon. Below the guideway grazed a herd of pronghorn antelope. She pinged their stats. Optimal gravidity, health a few points suboptimal but within the healthy range, immune systems boosted to counter the late-winter nutrient variance. This particular herd's population had been stable for a decade. They were the pride and joy of a wildlife biologist Minh knew from Tuk-U, a fat baby who'd taken over the breeding program from the biologist who'd initiated it forty years earlier. She trapped a minute of doc and shot it to him.

To their left, the Bow River sliced through dun prairie,

a silver ribbon curving into the foothills. Beyond, the mountain peaks glowed in the morning light.

As they approached the front ranges of the Rockies, the snowpack turned patchy. Minh's stomach flipped. She wiped the standard snowpack reports off her dashboard and dived into the guts of the live monitors. She threw fresh data across the horizon and drilled down into it, pedaling hard.

Five minutes later, she'd convinced herself the snowpack was fine. The patchiness was a trick of the light. Still, she had to rest her elbows on the handlebars and hang her head to get her blood pressure under control.

One season of low snowpack would put Calgary in a difficult position. They'd either have to evacuate half their population or install water printers. If they chose evacuation, only true surfacers like Minh would return, and the hab would be a ghost town. But installing water printers, like the Bank of Calgary wanted, would betray their ambitions and values. True surfacers would move to Iceland or Cusco, leaving Calgary to become a wart on a devastated landscape.

They exited the main guideway onto a private drive a few kilometers into the Kananaskis Valley, where the prairie rucked up into the peaks and crags of the continent's spine. The first blades of grass poked through the brown spruce and pine needles underfoot, and the chilly air brought a promise of fresh-flowing sap from the buds on the trembling aspen.

"We have to walk from here?" said Kiki.

"What's the problem?" asked Minh. "There's no predator alert. Ping the monitors if you're nervous."

"There's no people here. It's spooky."

A camera disk flew out of the trees and hovered overhead. Minh waved at its red eye.

"There's your people," she said.

They followed the camera up a wide bush trail.

"Can I ask what happened to your legs?" Kiki said. "Do you mind?"

"Ringworm. I was born in Sudbury Hell. The pandemics hit us hard," said Minh.

"The plagues were eighty years ago. You were just a crechie?"

"We didn't have crèches back then. We were all live births. With parents. Families."

"Do you remember walking?"

"I'm walking now." Minh smiled.

"You know what I mean."

She shook her head. "I remember the evacuation to Bangladesh Hell, the surgeries, and learning to use my first prostheses. They were dumb things, mechanical joints, completely inert. Huge advances in prosthesis tech since then. I've used these for ten years. I love them.

Everyone should have six legs."

"Why not eight? If it's an octopus, I mean."

Minh flapped her arms and wiggled her fingers. "These make eight."

A small skip rose silently toward the clouds, an elongated rose-colored egg riding a slim beam of power made visible by the angle of the morning sun—the iridescent condensation trail formed by the slight change in air pressure triggered by waste heat.

When they crested the ridge, Kananaskis Ranch stretched across the wide valley. A small hab gleamed like a diamond, surrounded by a cluster of antique outbuildings—stables and barns rebuilt on ancient stone foundations. Horses grazed in paddocks and pastures. Cattle topped the distant ridge, grazing on the dry grass at the edge of the ranch's boundary, where thick invasive scrub was forced back by a battery of specialized bots.

Kiki boggled. "Is this a . . . a farm?"

"It's a biodiversity reserve."

"People live like this?"

"Private banks can, if they want. Most stay underground."

As they approached the outbuildings, Hamid led a leggy young horse out of the stable, controlling it with a gentle, practiced hand. He walked the skittish animal around in a circle, paying out the lead line until the horse was orbiting him at a distance. By the time Minh and Kiki got close enough to hear hoofbeats and smell the grassy stench of horse manure, the animal looked relaxed, head down, ears up. Minh and Kiki leaned on the fence. Hamid ignored them, his focus on the tall beast at the end of the line.

Hamid's showing off, Minh whispered.

Is this safe? He's so tiny. The horse is a lot bigger than him.

There's nothing small about Hamid.

Hamid worked the horse into a steady canter for a few minutes, then slowed it to a walk and led it to meet them at the fence. Kiki gingerly stroked the animal's velvet nose.

"Aren't you a fat baby!" Hamid said, looking up at Kiki through the rails of the fence. "What was your birth weight?"

"Nearly 3,300 grams," said Kiki. "You?"

"Oh, me? You won't be impressed. I wasn't very viable. Surprised I survived at all. I'm a plague baby, you know. A dying breed. We're all getting old."

"You don't look old," Kiki said with all the loyalty of a best friend.

It wasn't a complete lie. Hamid still had his strong, flexible jockey physique, but his face showed as much wear and tear as Minh's. More, maybe.

"Is this ranch yours?" Kiki asked.

"Nah. I only live here." He gave Minh an icy glare and added, "For the moment. If Byron kicks me out, I'll be sleeping on Minh's floor."

"Did you read the RFP?" Minh asked.

"Does it matter? You put me on the team anyway. Did you want to ruin my life? You know the banks blab to each other. Gossipy as a crèche gang in puberty."

Kiki laughed. Hamid gave her an approving glance.

"Calgary told Iceland, Iceland told Cusco, Cusco told Zurich, and five minutes later, I'm in the middle of a domestic earthquake. Crockery flying everywhere, sturm and drang and betrayal and tears. And poor me standing in the middle, wondering what was going on."

"If you'd check your queue once in a while—"

"My queue is full. You're not the only one who wants a piece of me, Minh."

Now even Kiki was giving her a cold eye. She was on Hamid's side already—instant best friends. Hamid was four times her age and they had nothing in common, but Hamid could charm the skin off a snake.

Minh waited while Hamid stormed on. She'd known him since childhood. No point interrupting until he finished his grand performance.

When he finally wound down, Minh said, "I can drop you from the team—"

Kiki jumped into the fray. "I'll explain it was my mistake. I could say you refused, but I forgot."

Hamid smiled. "Sweet little fat baby, you're so kind. But I've already agreed to join the team."

She blinked. "You have?"

"Maybe Minh should check her queue once in a while."

Kiki rounded on Minh, braids flying.

Minh checked her queue. The message was there, marked low-priority and time-stamped to the exact moment she'd left Calgary. She shot it to Kiki.

Kiki looked confused. "All it says is 'Fine.'"

"Did I forget to include the material I trapped for the proposal? Here it is."

Hamid fired a doc into the middle of the corral, and they all watched two minutes and twenty seconds of skillfully edited biography emphasizing Hamid's multi-disciplinary reach in wildlife biology, veterinary science, and biodiversity field research.

"You only get a minute and a half," said Minh.

"I tried, my dear. But it just doesn't fit."

~

Hamid invited them into the hab. They sat in the middle of the atrium, on antique wooden benches. The overhead canopy of temperate greenery scented the air with spruce sap. The water feature's cascade pattered tunefully, an undercurrent to the chirping birds.

"Nobody's here," said Hamid. "Half the staff ran off to Calgary when the fight started, and the rest scattered to the edges of the ranch. Then Byron took the skip to Zurich."

"All this space." Kiki gaped.

"Disgusting, isn't it? I bet you've never seen so much empty hab. Calgary's packed tight. Last time I was there, I came home with three detanked infants hanging from my back. Had to get them lasered off."

Kiki laughed. "I'm from Jasper. It's not quite as bad there."

"So, Minh, what's your strategy?"

Minh stretched out on her bench, making herself comfortable. "We'll win it with the value-add."

"Uh-huh. That's what everyone says."

"Restoring the Tigris and Euphrates doesn't make a lot of sense. Mesopotamian climatic and flood patterns have always been unpredictable. West Asia has plenty of viable watersheds. If I were a private bank, I'd choose the Indus River. It flooded on a regular seasonal cycle, and the valley supported a huge population for thousands of years. So, there must be another reason. A sentimental reason."

"It's the cradle of civilization," said Kiki.

"One of them," amended Minh. "The client is fixated on

Mesopotamia. This is their passion project, so we'll make them an offer they can't refuse. Time travel is restricted by volume. We'll take up as little space as possible and offer them the rest for whatever they want—artifact retrieval, tourism, a side project. Or maybe they'll sell the space back to TERN for their own research."

"A small team." Hamid nodded. "Smart."

"You're a triple threat. You've got three disciplines sewn up—"

"And I'm remarkably svelte."

"I cover water, plants, geology, and project management. That gives us flexibility with the third team member."

"Entomologist, maybe. I won't do bugs. There's no winning against them."

Trust Hamid to cut right to the main problem.

"I know," Minh said. "The arthropod survey is huge. It would take a year to make a start. So, let's not try. We can use automated sampling for the bugs and hope the client doesn't realize how important they are."

"Do we need a third member at all?"

"Yes, or it looks like we're not serious."

"A research assistant, then."

Kiki jumped in. "I'd make a great research assistant. I have three years' admin experience, a crèche concentration in biology, and I can run a fab."

"No, Kiki. This strategy requires someone small. Minimum volume."

"You're not small," she said. "Your legs take up lots of room."

"They compress." Minh demonstrated, rolling her toe into a tight bundle.

"The bank likes me." Kiki's voice rose. "Succession planning, remember?"

Minh looked to Hamid for help.

"Private banks don't care about hab population dynamics." He patted Kiki's knee. "I'm sorry, but Minh's right. A small team is probably the only unique value-add we can offer."

The corners of her eyes reddened, but after a moment, Kiki nodded.

Minh wouldn't have blamed Kiki if she'd withdrawn after being rejected. But instead, she stayed fully engaged all afternoon, making helpful suggestions for possible third team members and sending off queries. She turned quiet on the ride home, though, lagging behind as if she were tired. When they returned to Minh's studio, she started packing.

"I'm taking a few days off," she said, stuffing clothes into her backpack. "A temp will cover my admin work."

Minh crossed her arms. "What about the full-time hours? Your debt?"

"My sections of the proposal are drafted, right? You signed off on them."

Minh nodded. Kiki ran out the door, backpack swinging from one shoulder.

I'll be back for the final edit, Kiki whispered. *Don't worry. I'm going to help you win this.*

7

SHULGI WOULD DIE TO protect his people. He would die to keep his borders strong. He would die if the gods willed it. But he wouldn't die because Susa disliked him.

When Susa announced her decision, Shulgi's household was shocked—his soldiers enraged, his wives red-faced and ball-fisted with fury, their children crying, his new wife tearful. She had already been once a widow.

Shulgi let them rage. Even as Susa threatened to spill his blood down the steps, he had to stay impassive, regal, obedient to the gods. He let his people speak his anger for him.

~

A temp ran the Monday morning meeting. He stuck close to the agenda, hitting all the talking points and reports Kiki usually skipped.

What did you do to Kiki? David whispered. *If we have to find a new admin, I'm tapping you to lead the search.*

Minh let her fake answer.

A few days later, Kiki wheeled through Minh's door in a blue bumper chair. Kiki's legs were gone, short stumps sealed under polymer caps studded with shunts and drains that threaded into the body of the chair. A life-support goiter thrummed under her jaw.

Minh sat on the sofa so hard it cracked.

"Kiki, I . . ." She searched for the words. "What did you do?"

"Nothing different from you. Except you were just a crechie."

Kiki's voice was raw, as if she'd been screaming. Her complexion was ashen, bloodless as charcoal, her bright smile a fading spark.

"Are you . . ." The words came out high and quivery. *Completely insane,* she thought. *Worse than insane. Stupid and destructive and wrong.*

"Am I what?" Kiki's hands lay in her lap, quaking gently like dying things.

Minh looked away.

"Did it hurt?" she said.

Such a stupid, useless question. Trite. Unforgivable. She was probably the first person to say it to Kiki. She'd hear it again and again, over and over for the rest of her life, and she'd always remember Minh had been the first to say it.

"Yeah," Kiki answered, her voice flat and dull. "Not

too bad, though. I have a medtech on pain management and recovery monitoring. You're supposed to review the work protocols for staff in medical recovery."

Minh nodded. If she kept her mouth shut, she wouldn't make any more mistakes.

"If the pain intervention causes a seizure, this will intervene." She patted the arm of the chair. "I'm back to work now. And I'll be full speed on prostheses by the time the project starts."

"What project?" Minh asked. Kiki wasn't making sense.

Kiki's skin was thin and dry, drawn tight at the corners of her mouth.

"I'm resident in Calgary now. The bank bought my debt from Jasper, so I'm starting fresh with Calgary credit. If we win the project, they'll zero it out and I'll be debt free. For a while, anyway."

"What project?" Minh repeated.

She wanted to take Kiki by the shoulders and shake her. Instead, she curled her legs around the base of the sofa and squeezed. The frame shifted, cracking again. Kiki didn't seem to notice.

"The bank wants me on the team. I guess they liked your projection numbers."

Minh winced. Kiki had mutilated herself because of imaginary numbers—numbers Minh had made up.

"Where's Hamid?" Kiki asked. "I need to talk to both of you."

Kiki flicked a shaking hand. Hamid's fake appeared in the middle of the studio. Hat, chaps, and all.

Override, Minh told it. *Hamid, get here right now. Emergency. No fucking fakes.*

The fake's cheesy costume faded. Its blank expression blossomed into a grin as Hamid took over. He opened his mouth, then caught sight of Kiki.

His face fell.

"Oh, Kiki. Your perfect fat baby body. What did you do?"

"What I had to." Kiki backed up her chair and faced them both. "In addition to my admin experience and crèche-level biology, I'm a fabrication technologist with more than four thousand hours of experience fabbing construction components in Jasper."

She shot Minh's draft work plan into the center of the room. A blue-highlighted constellation of items flashed as they scrolled by.

"The work breakdown is swarming with fab tasks," she said. "People think fabbing is brainless work. They think you can load a recipe and walk away, but you can't. It's not as easy as it looks, especially on a tight deadline. Efficient fab management requires attention and experience."

The bumper chair beeped softly. Kiki fished a pouch of hydration fluid out of a cubby in the arm rest, poked a straw through its seal, and sipped.

"More importantly," she continued, "Minh and I work well together in close quarters. I'm completely dedicated to the success of the project. I'll do anything to make it work. I think I've proved that."

Hamid's eyes glimmered. Minh turned to the window and wiped the sleeve of her coverall over her damp brow.

"You both think I'm crazy," Kiki said. "I'm not. I'm fine. All I did was exercise autonomy over my health decisions, like you plague babies do." Kiki forced her pained smile brighter. "My volume is now slightly less than one and a half cubic meters. I want to be on this team, Minh. I'm willing to do whatever it takes."

Minh scrubbed her palms over her eyes.

"Why didn't you tell me?" she said. It came out a whine.

"Tell you what?" Hamid snarled. "What did you want her to say? 'Put me on the team or I'll cut my legs off'? You'd have told David to fire her. But now you have no choice. You *have* to put her on the team." He dashed away the tears and grinned. "It's diabolical, Kiki. I'm proud of you."

"What if we don't win?" asked Minh.

"Then we'll win the next one," said Kiki. "Life is long."

~

Kiki offered to get a sleep stack, but Minh wasn't going to let her rack up debt renting space by the hour. She mulched her sofa to make room for Kiki's chair. Minh liked sleeping in the hammock, and the sofa's frame was beyond repair, anyway.

The day after they delivered the proposal, Kiki started rehab. She wheeled out of the studio in the mornings, dragged herself back home six hours later to do a little admin work, and then fell into sleep so deep it looked like death.

Kiki's spirits climbed as she recovered, but Minh's plunged. All her regular project work felt dull in comparison to the time travel project. Repetitive, pointless reiterations and reexaminations of ecological management decisions made thirty or forty years earlier. Did Iceland really need another review of a successful valley restoration project, or were they throwing Calgary a bone? Did Cusco really want a resculpt of their glacier field, or were her friends trying to keep her busy?

Iceland had fifty restored valleys. Cusco's glaciers were constantly on the move. Minh couldn't face the idea of repeating the same projects for the rest of her life just to prove her value to the Bank of Calgary.

Instead of logging billable hours, she updated her old

Tuk-U lectures. She sent a battery of cameras up the Bow River to trap fresh doc footage to supplement her simulation models and demonstration materials. And she worried about Kiki. Every hour, Minh pinged Kiki's biom to confirm she hadn't hemorrhaged out.

Each time, Kiki's biom was the same—green-alive. But between green-alive and red-dead was a world of pain. She knew what Kiki was going through.

Minh's blood pressure swung wildly, far worse than usual. When one of her teratomas sprung a bleed, Minh's medtech claimed the problem wasn't entirely physiological and recommended a therapist. The fourth time the medtech mentioned therapy, Minh fired her.

Minh ignored her project deadlines until the last minute, and delivered the final reports late. When Iceland offered her a set of new adaptive management reviews, she forwarded them to David.

I need a break, she told him.

Minh retreated to Crowchild Terrace and finished pruning the entire orchard herself.

When the interview notice arrived from the Mesopotamian Development Bank, Kiki was away at a medical engineering appointment, having her training prostheses installed. As Minh fired the client an acknowledgement, her blood pressure soared, then plunged. Minh nearly passed out. She climbed into her hammock, pulled her legs into a tight ball, and waited.

Kiki tottered through the door on two squat, thick training prostheses and grinned up at her.

"I'm shorter than you now," she said. Then she checked the queue and fired the notice into the middle of the studio, triumphant.

Minh burrowed deeper into her hammock and watched the client's administrative fake deliver the message. Minh's biom surged into the red. Blood pressure through the ceiling. Pinpoint hemorrhages in her liver and esophagus. If Minh hadn't dismissed her medtech, the situation would already be under control. Now, if she wanted medical assistance, she'd have to ask for it. But she hated asking for help.

"They want us to interview in Bangladesh Hell," Kiki said. "Amazing. You know I've never been anywhere?"

Prostheses clanged on the floor as Kiki danced around the studio.

"Interview notices are always so dispassionate. They never really say anything. It's like they don't want you to get your hopes up. And what's up with that admin fake? Face like a dinner plate."

"I don't know." Minh turned toward the window and fixed her gaze on the cold mountains in the distance. "I guess it's a custom design."

"We're going to win, you know."

"Maybe."

Kiki laughed. "Come on. Aren't you excited?"

Minh lowered herself to the floor and scuttled into the bathroom.

"What do we do now?" Kiki shouted through the door.

Minh pretended not to hear.

Small bleed in her left sphenoid sinus. Her cheekbone burned as clotting agents rushed in to stop the flow. A drop of blood splattered on the tiles, then another on the edge of the shower drain. If she didn't control her blood pressure, she'd pop a thrombosis. And with no medtech agreement in place, it'd be a quick slide from palliative care to the mulch.

Minh reached into her biom and tweaked her hormonal mix, dialing herself down until a cold calm settled over her like a new skin.

It was a dangerous habit, hard on the endocrine system. For most of Minh's life, she'd tweaked the dials compulsively, unable to resist the temptation to optimize her state of mind—control moods, enhance concentration, keep alert, awake, and productive. For a long time, it worked, but years of abuse had damaged her angiotensin and aldosterone response, making her blood pressure wildly irregular.

When her diagnosis had been finalized, Minh's

medtech had yelled at her for twenty minutes straight. All Minh could do was listen and nod. She'd hurt herself. Badly.

So, she'd stopped playing with her endocrine system. Hadn't touched the dials in nearly two years. Probably shouldn't now, but she needed it. She had to stay under control.

Minh slathered cleansing cream on her face and scoured it off with steady hands. Her biom flashed green.

She stared at herself in the mirror, poking at the pouches under her eyes with a fingertip. She was okay. Next time she got a bleed, she'd let a professional deal with it. Nothing in Minh's life was going to change because a fat baby made an impulse decision on a body mod.

When she left the bathroom, Kiki was talking with Hamid.

"Getting the interview is nothing," he said. "The short-list includes at least three teams."

Kiki laughed. "You can't say that. It's not nothing!"

"If we don't win, how much debt will you have in six months?" Kiki looked away. "Right. So, here's your first interview question: Kiki, why do you want to time travel?"

Kiki didn't even think before answering, "Who wouldn't want to time travel? It's the ultimate adventure."

"Zero points." Hamid turned to Minh. "Why do you want to time travel?"

"The Mesopotamian ecological system is the foundational habitat for the development of modern human societies," Minh said, falling into standard interview mode. Confident but deferential, completely trustworthy. "In my sixty years as an ecological remediation specialist, this project is unprecedented. It provides a unique opportunity to take the first concrete step in restoring an ecosystem using past-state data observed, monitored, and gathered on-site."

"Good. You see what Minh did there?"

Kiki shook her head.

"Minh told the client they have the prettiest gonads and she's the best possible person to bring their project off. Want to try again?"

Kiki stumped around the studio, thinking.

"I'm at the beginning of my life," Kiki said, finally. "When time travel became a reality, I was in the crèche. Over the past ten years, time travel has been used for a lot of things, but it's never been used for the most important work of all—restoring productive ecosystems so they can support the population growth my generation represents. This project is the first step."

Hamid coughed. Kiki backtracked. "This project will prove past-state monitoring is the best and highest possible use of time travel technology."

"Not bad," Hamid said. "Stay away from the me-me-me. Clients want you to talk about them."

"I didn't realize we needed to make the client feel good about themselves. It seems dishonest."

"This is a seduction," Hamid said. "If you want to time travel, we need to get the client in bed with us."

8

BEFORE SHULGI LEFT THE temple, he had to perform the parting ritual. Shulgi took Susa's hand, as was his duty, and Susa led him to Inanna's bed, as was her duty. There, they honored the gods. Shulgi swallowed his anger and put as much reverence into the act as he could muster. Susa made no attempt to bridle her hatred. With her nails and teeth, she drew as much blood from him as she could.

Meanwhile, Shulgi's eldest wife argued with the priests. She was a former moon priestess, gray-haired and venerable, a practiced orator who knew all the weaknesses and foibles in the temple precincts. The priests agreed to wait for more signs, more portents.

They didn't have to wait long.

~

Minh, Hamid, and Kiki skipped from Calgary to Iceland, Iceland to Surgut, then Surgut to Bangladesh. From hab to hab to hive to hell.

Minh hadn't skipped in years. She'd forgotten how much she enjoyed the weightlessness, the delight of escaping gravity. She let her limbs float, and strain bubbled out of her hips and spine.

Kiki had only seen habs she could visit by bike—Edmonton, Jasper, Calgary, Moberly, Tsay Keh Dene. She'd never seen a hive or hell. Skip travel was all new to her—from the elongated egg-like skip hull nestled into its cushioned pad, to its soft, spongy, noise-absorbing interior, to the bioresponsive seats lining the bulkheads. When they hit apogee, Kiki squealed like a toddler crechie. Her excitement was infectious. Minh and most of the other passengers grinned.

Hamid slept through it all. In Iceland, he yawned as he crawled out of the skip.

"What's wrong with you?" Kiki asked. "How could you sleep through the flight?"

"If I had to guess," said Minh, "I'd say Hamid spent last night reconciling with Byron."

Hamid draped an arm across Kiki's shoulders. "Don't listen to gossip. It's beneath you," he said in a stage whisper, and then added in a loud voice, as if announcing it to the whole hab, "I heard most fat babies have never had fish."

Minh grimaced. "Calgary won't fund fresh food in Iceland. Our trade deficit is too wide."

"My treat," he said, and then amended, "Byron's treat. Just enough time if we hurry."

The moment they crossed the hab's diamond-faceted skip-pad doors and stepped onto the speeding slideway, the lower third of Minh's eye began scrolling with dashboards. Health, mortality, conflict resolution, operating budget, hab component life cycle, emergency response, nutrition, trade development, training and education—two hundred dashes in total.

When the ecological restoration dash floated by, Minh drilled down into it. Sure enough, her latest adaptive management review was posted. More than two hundred people had already accessed it.

Hamid led them into an atrium so crowded with people, the floor pulsed like a heartbeat.

"Am I doing something wrong?" Kiki waved her hand in front of her eyes. "I can't dismiss this info stream."

"It's not optional in Iceland. Here, they demand complete information transparency," Hamid said. "That's how Iceland hooks you. Once you get used to having every bit of data at your fingertips, you can't go without. Icelanders want to know everything."

They rode an elevator to the apex of the hab and claimed a table in a glass spire overlooking the slate-gray ocean. Waves stippled the water's surface. White gulls whirled and spun in the buffeting wind, each bird marked with a glowing green datapoint.

Kiki pressed her nose to the glass.

"The Open Ocean dashboard says Iceland hasn't experienced an algae-mat bloom in over a year. Is that good or bad? I can't tell."

"I'd say it's so-so," Hamid answered.

Minh shrugged. "I'm a freshwater specialist. Oceans are a foreign discipline."

A bot brought their order—three baskets of crispy fried smelts, crusted with salt and accompanied by tubs of garlic sauce.

Kiki crunched a finger-sized fish, her eyes half-closed with pleasure.

"I think I could put up with Iceland's info stream if I could eat these anytime I wanted."

"It's tempting," Minh agreed.

"Don't talk. Eat," said Hamid.

They wolfed the meal and ran to catch the next stage of their trip.

On the downskip into Surgut, Minh glanced at the skip's live feed. More than half the landscape was obscured with billowing smoke. Only one reach of the Ob River was visible, a slender braid of green and silver threads in the dry Siberian taiga.

Kiki was glued to the feed.

I have friends down there, she whispered. *They left to join the Siberian hives as soon as we got out of the crèche.*

Minh flicked on the underground overlay. Surgut appeared as a glowing network of tiny beads along the course of the river, with slender tendrils spreading out in every direction to meet the fires.

Are they going to come see you? Minh asked.

A shadow passed over Kiki's face.

No. I asked. They all said they're too busy.

The hives discourage contact with outsiders.

Kiki forced a smile. *People in the habs don't talk about Surgut much.*

The banks hate the hives because they don't participate in the economy. And the plague babies don't talk about them because they put us all to shame. We like to think we're the most virtuous people on the planet, but the hives sacrifice everything fighting those underground fires.

After landing in Surgut, they climbed down into a long cell with open bunks, hard benches, and a grimy extruder station. The other passengers pulled bikes off a rack and dispersed out the guideway port. The three of them waited for the next leg alone.

Kiki wandered over to the port and looked up and down the guideway.

"It's a ghost town. Worse than Edmonton. Where are all the people?"

Hamid settled back on a bench and closed his eyes.

"Wait for Bangladesh," he said. "Then you'll be impressed."

They landed in Bangladesh Hell hundreds of feet belowground, on a multipad platform teeming with activity—elevators and guideways, tunnels and chutes, bots and fakes, passengers and gawkers, and above it all, the silent skips gently rising and falling.

Bangladesh dominated more economic sectors than any other hell. Two hundred years earlier, when faced with rising sea levels, they had been the first to tunnel deep into the earth's crust and carve new frontiers out of rock. When the fires, storms, and floods hit, Bangladesh's tunneling tech was already in place, along with the expertise to make humanity's retreat underground successful. When the plagues began spreading, Bangladesh's experience managing public health in highly concentrated populations provided the systems and expertise to deal most effectively with the outbreaks. They shared their expertise in that crisis, too.

It hadn't been charity. It was a long-term investment in leadership and human capital that paid off globally.

A beautiful fake led Minh, Hamid, and Kiki through a series of vaulted, intricately carved, dramatically lit atria. Minh knew Bangladesh. She'd guest lectured at U-Bang twice and had attended several of their academic conferences, but still, she felt assaulted by the unrelenting sensory input—noise, unfamiliar scents of food, spices, and perfumes circulated by the breath of millions. Hamid still looked droopy-eyed and sleepy. In stark contrast, Kiki looked worried, almost scared. Her left hand plucked at the join of her stumpy prosthesis.

Kiki clutched the slideway rail.

"I'm not used to being so short. I feel like someone's going to step on me."

The fake flashed a dazzling smile. "When you're ready to upgrade your training prostheses, I can recommend several custom design studios. The Bank of Bangladesh would be happy to negotiate terms with the Bank of Calgary on your behalf."

"Hah, no, thanks. I'd never pay it off." Kiki dismissed the fake. "The Mesopotamian Development Bank did this on purpose, didn't they? They don't need to interview us face-to-face. Making us come here is part of their strategy. They want us to feel small."

Hamid's eyes snapped wide, suddenly alert. "I don't feel small," he said. "I'm exactly the right size, and everyone else is sadly stretched."

"Clients like to display their economic power," Minh said. "Make sure we know they're rich and important. And if they lease an office in Bangladesh, they are rich. I bet Byron doesn't have an office here."

"No," Hamid said. "He prefers Calgary. The views are nicer."

"Byron can't afford Bangladesh. But apparently this client can."

Hamid led them to a tiny café overlooking a saltwater cascade. Below, kayakers shot rapids and sieves, spun and flipped through boils and whirlpools. The rocks forming the artificial river were topped with thick shells of white salt, like gleaming mushrooms. Minh sat with her back to the river so she wouldn't get distracted critiquing the flow design. They drank coffee and nibbled biscotti as they reviewed their interview plan, and then arrived at the client's office with a few minutes to spare.

The bank's platter-faced fake pinged their IDs. Acoustic shielding closed behind them, replacing the crowd noise with a velvet silence. It invited them to sit in a high-ceilinged, thick-carpeted boardroom filled with antiquities, and offered them beverages.

Load your interview prompts, Minh whispered.

Over the previous three days, the three of them had crafted thoughtful answers to the standard and expected interview questions, plus a few dozen trick questions concocted by Minh's partners. They'd trapped the responses and sent the doc to a client-relations consultant who edited the responses complete with tone, intonation, and pauses optimized to achieve maximum effect. They'd even thrown in regional dialect mitigation as a value-add.

Each response was indexed with an adaptive keyword scheme to supply the optimal answer to any question the client could ask. The tactic turned interviews into orchestrated live performances—concocted and completely artificial. Minh hated it, but she couldn't deny the results. The simple fact was, she won more jobs parroting optimal answers than honestly extemporizing an interview.

If Minh had to jump through hoops to win contracts, she was resigned to it. A necessary evil.

Three cameras flew into place, hovering overhead, and the admin fake began asking questions. After a few minutes, the door opened and a pointy-nosed man entered the room, silent and anonymous, his ID under veil except for his name—Fabian. When Minh paused and offered him a professional half-smile, he motioned for her to continue. He padded across the carpet and sat in a leather chair between two antiquities, a lion statue in painted terra-cotta, its colors faded and subdued, and the golden head of a bull, its forelock, beard, and the tips of its horns carved in violet stone.

Is he the client? whispered Kiki.

Looks like a junior admin, replied Hamid. *Probably a procurement consultant overseeing the interview feed.*

At least we have a real person to talk to now, whispered Minh.

But when Minh answered the next question, she found herself playing to the lion and the bull instead of Fabian. Their expressions were warmer, more alive.

After the interruption, the interview proceeded as planned. Minh's role was professional gravitas, making the most of her age and senior consultant experience. Kiki bubbled with enthusiasm and energy, while Hamid played hard to get. His part of the performance was key, adding the intrigue and mystery that implied the client would get much more than they bargained for. It was irresistible—should have been irresistible, anyway, to any human.

Fabian watched them perform, his eyes expressionless, insectile. After an hour of fake-fed questions, Minh's professional detachment began to fray. She half-hated him while he remained silent and judgmental, but her dislike was confirmed the instant he opened his mouth.

"That's enough questions." Fabian dismissed the fake and fired a logic puzzle onto the table. "Could you complete this teamwork task, please?"

Hamid laughed. Minh ignored the prompt that supplied her with a diplomatic refusal.

"This is basic-level testing," she said. "It's demeaning. Our team is backed by a reputable ecological sciences firm. Our references and recommendations were included with our proposal."

Fabian slapped down the test.

"Fine," he said. "Your team can qualify for the job. It doesn't mean you should get it. What do you know about time travel?"

Minh recognized his clipped accent. Five years back, when Calgary abandoned the University of Tuktoyaktuk and let CEERD lease the entire hab, the incoming population had sounded like Fabian.

He's not a procurement consultant, Minh whispered. *He's from TERN.*

Time to take a gamble. Minh ignored her prompt and went off script.

"How could we know anything about time travel? TERN never tells anyone anything. But I know one thing for certain. You've never taken a restoration ecology team into the past."

Fabian's look of surprise told Minh she'd guessed right. Her courage soared.

"If TERN already had a relationship with an experienced team," she said, "the bank would be working with them instead of putting this RFP out to public call."

He smiled. His teeth were small, evenly spaced implants, bright white and gleaming.

"This project will require your team to spend three weeks in isolation. Have you ever been completely alone before?" he asked.

"I was born during the plagues," Minh said. "Of course I've been alone."

He turned to Hamid, who looked disdainful and declined to answer. Fabian turned to Kiki.

"What do the habs call your generation—fat babies? Crèches are highly problematic by the standards of most hells. In Bangladesh, they believe family is everything."

Kiki's smile was genuine, as if she hadn't even thought of taking offense.

"Maybe there's a better way to grow up, but I liked it. My upbringing makes me a good team member. I know how to contribute to a project without going diva and turning everything into a fight. A crèche teaches you how to cooperate."

"The fat babies are going to save the habs, are they?" Fabian smirked.

He was going out of his way to be obnoxious. Minh had seen it before; some clients liked to test a team's professionalism.

Easy, Minh whispered. *He's baiting you.*

"It's true, I've never really been alone," Kiki said. "But if you choose our team for this project, I'll have Minh and Hamid with me. The three of us work well together."

"I'll be working with you, too," he said. "Whichever consultant team the bank chooses, I'll be part of it. Any objections?"

Minh's vision swam as her blood pressure plunged. *Hamid, take the question.*

She locked her gaze on the lion's faded eye, faking calm as she wrestled her body back under control with a few slow, deep breaths.

"That's the client's prerogative," Hamid said. "But we can't answer your question until we know more about you."

"I'm a TERN historian. My specialty is ancient history to classical antiquity. The client's target falls within that catchment."

He's a time traveler, Kiki whispered. *Imagine the stories he can tell.*

Fabian turned to Minh. "We'll be on-site for only three weeks. The rivers might not flood. How complete will your data be without a flood event?"

Minh parroted her canned response. "We can extrapolate information about flood seasons from the geophysical evidence on the floodplain, and even more from core sample analysis. We can model flood events using the data we collect."

"What if a flood started an hour before retrieval?" Fabian asked. "Wouldn't it bother you to leave that event behind unobserved and unrecorded?"

She didn't have a canned response prepared for that one, but it was easy enough to answer.

"Firsthand observation of a flood event would be interesting, but we're not traveling to the past for a tourist experience."

"I think that's the end of the bank's questions." Fabian's eyes glazed for a moment. "Yes, they say they're done. But I'd like to ask a few of my own questions, under a privacy veil, if you're willing."

Fabian fired a veil request onto the table.

As Minh's stream dropped behind the veil, she realized she was slouching. She rearranged her legs, sat a little taller. It had been a long day. She was stiff. Her back ached with tension and her blood pressure was spiraling. Her biom was compensating with increased heart rate, but the pressor response was sluggish. Not good. She had to stay sharp. Alert.

Minh reached into her biom, brought up the hormonal balance dash, and dialed a little adrenaline. Her vision snapped into focus and her fingers tingled with the urge to fidget.

Fabian rose from the leather chair and joined them on their side of the conference table, sitting with his elbows on his knees, hands open.

"You guessed right, Minh," he said. "TERN's never considered ecological restoration projects. We've never seen the point. I mean—the resurfacing movement is dead, isn't it?"

Minh bit off a pointed reply. "Not at all. Studies show the habs are in a temporary lull. Economic recovery is projected within the next decade. Humanity will reclaim our ancestral habitats. Your client obviously believes that, too, or they wouldn't be initiating this project."

Fabian shrugged. "TERN doesn't care whether our clients' projects make sense. If they want us to do a job, we find a way to get it done. But now I'm wondering if environmental studies could open a new area of business for us. Do you think this project is a viable use of time travel?"

"Ecological baseline studies and current-state assessments are a fundamental part of ecological restoration. I can't tell you if it's cost-effective, because it's never been done before. But if you want to know what kind of return on investment it could provide, I could give TERN a quote for a study."

At a very high hourly rate, she thought.

"Perhaps after this project." Fabian dropped the privacy veil. "We're at the end of our time. Any last questions?"

Minh jumped in with a scripted question David had concocted to underline the team's strengths.

Fabian interrupted her mid-script. "Any real questions?"

"What do you think of our work plan?" Minh asked. "Is it realistic?"

He applied the veil again before answering.

"You'll have to revise it. We can't stay on the ground in Mesopotamia the whole three weeks. It's not safe."

"What can you tell us about TERN's mortality rates?" Hamid asked.

"Health and safety is TERN's first priority. We do everything possible to protect our people in the past. Experienced time travelers have the rarest skill set on the planet. Protecting that resource base is in our best interest."

"TERN will guarantee our safety?" Minh asked.

"TERN will," he said. "And so will I."

9

THE NEW STARS BROUGHT trouble. Reports of monsters and spirits cropped up whenever Shulgi's people were nervous about the future, but these were real omens. Three swans plunged from the sky and impaled themselves on a grape trellis. At the same time, an amber egg appeared in a barley field north of Asnear, and whatever hatched from within murdered six soldiers and flew away before it could be confronted.

When Shulgi's falconers talked to the field workers who had witnessed everything, they reported four monsters. Accompanying them were flying spirits: silver stones with single red eyes, gray slabs edged with hornet stripes, and a head-sized black burr that turned soldiers into unblemished corpses.

~

On the upskip to Surgut, Kiki searched for data on Fabian. He was from a CEERD family line, the child of a senior economist who'd spent the past two decades seconded to the World Economic Council. Fabian had qualifications in history and linguistics. He'd been with TERN since his undergrad degree.

"If he thinks he can boss me around, he'll learn different pretty quick," Hamid said as they waited in Surgut. "I've been riding two-year-old colts my whole life. They all think they're number one on the track."

"All those advanced degrees," said Kiki. "It's pretty intimidating."

"The degrees mean nothing." Minh felt the mattress of one of the Surgut bunks, wondering if it was as uncomfortable as it looked. She hoisted herself up and reclined. The plastic mattress cover squeaked. "Fabian's showing how superior he is, like everyone associated with CEERD."

Kiki shrugged. "He's not worse than you, Minh."

Minh lurched up and gaped at her.

"I was so scared of you my first year at ESSA," Kiki continued mildly, as if she hadn't just kicked Minh in the gut. "All business, so forbidding. You didn't need my help, not with anything. I couldn't buy a kind word, not even from your fake."

"I didn't know—"

"It's okay," Kiki interrupted, smiling. "I figured it out. You've seen it all before. Your life is optimized. You don't need random variables. When we first met, I was nobody.

Another admin. No better than a fake."

Minh jumped out of the bunk. "Kiki—"

"But for me it was different. I was so excited to get the job at ESSA. I thought if I worked hard and proved myself, you'd give me opportunities to learn and grow. I never minded being stuck in admin—running meetings, editing docs, managing the company message queue, doing everything for everyone. I knew someday I'd do important work."

Kiki's grin became luminous. "And I was right. We're going to time travel."

She fired the award notice into the middle of the cell. A flashing alert showed the Bank of Calgary was already reviewing the contract.

Whispers poured in from partners, friends, and colleagues, congratulating Minh on the win. When the skip arrived to take them to Iceland, Minh was so busy juggling multiple streams, Kiki had to herd her across the pad and into her seat. Her queue filled with interview requests, not only from hab media but from all over the world—even a big Bangladesh feed. Minh set her fake on them all.

Back in Calgary, when the bank offered her a choice of new studios, she had her fake brush them off, too. Minh had more important things to do than play nice with media or move into a new space.

She had a long list of urgent and important tasks. David needed prep to take over her ongoing projects before they fell too far behind. But first, she needed to finalize the project inventory so the equipment would arrive on time. Technically, she couldn't do that before revising the time travel work plan, but the revision would take days and the equipment had to be ordered immediately. Cart before the horse—equipment before work plan. She sped through the inventory as quickly as she could, making educated guesses and pulling numbers out of thin air. Kiki and Hamid handled the procurement and logistics, ordering sampling tech from Calgary, satellites from Iceland, and cameras from Cusco while she fine-tuned the work plan according to notes forwarded by TERN.

A week later, Minh, Hamid, and Kiki were the only passengers on a direct skip to TERN, billable from the moment they strapped into their seats. They downskipped into a high alpine valley, the mountains furred over with invasive scrub. Minh couldn't tell the exact location. TERN had required them to accept a block on their geopositioning before leaving Calgary. Western Alps, she guessed.

When they landed, Fabian waited by the side of the pad, hands in the pockets of his gray coverall. Minh's dislike of him hadn't abated—his beady eyes, his nose sharp as a beak, his air of superiority—but she swallowed it. Considered dispassionately, she was happy to have him on the team. It meant she didn't have to think about basic project logistics.

She forced herself to be sincere, look him in the eyes, smile.

"Congratulations," he said. "Your team was my first choice. I'm glad the client agreed."

He led them to an elevator. "You'll stay in medical for the two-day prep phase, then join me in pre-launch. While you're in medical, you'll need to review the project protocol. It's a bit tedious, but TERN's project control standards support successful project outcomes." Fabian looked abstracted, eyes glazed.

"That sounds like a mission statement," Minh said.

"It is." Fabian's focus snapped back. "Sorry. I'm running multiple streams. Listen, Minh, you have an ambitious work plan but you know how to keep your team on top of it. Hamid, you're a cowboy. You need a loose rein and that's fine. But you—" He pinned Kiki with an intense glare. "You're the future. This project is for you. Make the most of it."

What a diva, Minh whispered to Kiki.

He's not wrong. Kiki grinned. *Aren't you excited?*

I'll let you know when I see something to get excited about.

Minh expected the roughhewn corridors to become

more polished as they descended under the mountain, but it never happened. The hell was utilitarian, with low ceilings, temporary shelving, sparse lighting, and flimsy, ill-fitting grill flooring. No effort spent on aesthetics.

Medical hit them with a barrage of tests and preventative interventions. Teeth, gums, gut flora, connective tissues, and endocrine and organ systems. Minh hated it, but she gritted her teeth and let the techs prod her.

Months back, Minh's medtech had bookmarked a twitchy heart valve. Minh had procrastinated, and now she had no choice but to let TERN take care of it. The twenty-minute procedure was supervised by a CEERD senior surgeon resident in Tuktoyaktuk. He was oversolicitous. Minh's fake fielded all his questions while Minh lurked, scowling so hard her jaw hurt.

She wasn't the only one the techs got their hands on. Kiki upgraded to full-size prostheses. Hamid had a procedure, too.

"It's private," he told Kiki when she asked about it. "As far as you know, I'm immortal."

Kiki showed off her new prostheses. "I wanted six legs like Minh, but turns out you can't add four additional limbs and expect to be able to control them right away. So, two legs for now."

She'd chosen an ungulate model, strong, adaptable, and sturdy. The sheaths matched Kiki's brown complexion, and the split-toe hooves were glossy black. Kiki flexed, crouched low, and then stretched high to slap the ceiling with her palms. At full extension, Kiki was even taller than before, and alarmingly clumsy.

"Most people who go with this design choose to cover it in fur," she said. "But that's for aesthetics."

"You'll spend a few days thinking about nothing else, but soon they'll be familiar as your arms," Minh said.

"A human ankle-knee-hip model would be easier to adapt to, but this joint design is superior for speed and stability."

Minh nodded. "Why be human when you can be more?"

Kiki backed against the wall, gripped one hoof in her hand, and examined the sole.

"The legs collapse for storage, like yours, but the hooves are solid. The split-toe design is pure goat. Hard hoof wall, soft sole, and dewclaw. Rock climbers like this model." She eyed the rough wall supporting the medical department mezzanine level. "I could probably climb this cavern if I wanted to." Then she dropped her hoof and nearly fell over. She laughed. "Maybe not for a while."

Minh dove into project-management mode. She wanted to skim through TERN's project protocol information and then focus on further refining her work plan using whatever historical information she could get access to. But the project protocol docs were tedious, with hour upon hour of real-time content. Summarizing and scanning ahead were disabled. Worse, at the end of each doc they were forced to complete tests before moving to the next.

When Fabian claimed them from medical, Minh was furious.

"I can't believe you made us do comprehension testing," Minh said. "Who do you usually travel with? Toddler crechies?"

Fabian ticked the answers off on his fingers as he led them into the elevator.

"Tourists. Collectors. Artists and artisans. Doc teams. Forensic economists from CEERD. Tactical teams. And historians, of course. Mostly TERN's strategic historians, but outsiders tag along if they have the funding. Usually, they have to attach themselves to an entertainment doc production team. They never complain about comprehension testing. They're grateful to get the chance to do real historical research."

Grateful, Minh whispered. *TERN destroyed an entire academic discipline, and he thinks historians should thank them for it.*

I'm grateful, Kiki whispered. *I feel lucky to get this chance.*

Hamid smirked as the elevator descended. *Go ahead,*

Minh. Give Fabian a piece of your mind. Get it over with.

Fabian leaned against the elevator's mesh walls, arms crossed, watching her closely. For a moment, Minh considered giving in to her worst impulses, let him have the full diva treatment. But no.

Get him out of my face before I tell him what he should be grateful for.

"Fabian, did the medical department contact you?" Kiki asked. "They bookmarked a pending issue."

Fabian scrubbed the back of his hand over his lips as he checked his queue. "They say you're refusing to transfer medical authority. That's a problem. Project protocol gives me access to all your bioms."

"It's a smart policy," Kiki said. "But protocol also says when there's a medical professional on the team, authority goes to them. And we have one."

"Veterinarians don't count."

"I'm a large mammal specialist," said Hamid. "Humans are large mammals."

Fabian threw his hands up. "I can't argue with that."

Kiki continued chatting as he led them through TERN's corridors.

"What's your specialty, Fabian?" asked Kiki. "Are you a strategic historian?"

"No. TERN's history operations are divided into two divisions—strategic and tactical. Strategic historians do research and planning. Tactical historians get the work done. That's me."

"I bet those two divisions fight like cats," said Hamid.

"Would a strategic historian make us waste time going through all those basic docs?" asked Minh.

Fabian spread his hands wide. "We have to spend three weeks together, Minh. Don't hold the project protocol against me."

"It's not personal," Minh said.

"You built Tuktoyaktuk, right? I was there for a CEERD conference a few months ago. It's nice. Tuk-U must have been a great little school."

Minh's blood pressure blasted into the red.

"I hope CEERD likes it. You have a long lease. But remember, aboveground, you're all simply tourists trying to remember what it's like to be human."

Fabian gave her a feral smile, teeth gleaming. "Are you sure it's not personal?"

The elevator doors opened and they all stepped out into a crowded hallway. Fabian led the way single file, talking over his shoulder at Minh. She avoided his eyes, seething.

"I know the docs are dull," he said. "But you're not the only one who's bored. I've been running package tours for weeks. Yesterday was twelve hours at Carnac. I've made that trip more than forty times."

"Isn't it dangerous, bringing tourists to the past?" asked Kiki.

"We only send package tours to established baselines, where we have decision support to cover every contingency."

"Sounds boring," said Hamid.

"The food is good. We bring along a chef," Fabian said. "But this is no package tour you're going on. Nobody has ever landed in 2024 BCE, not even me."

"Will you take tourists there, eventually?" asked Kiki.

"Maybe. If conditions are right. Not package tours, though, not right away. Private excursions first."

"You can repeat the trips over and over, and every time you leave, the timeline collapses," Kiki said. "But how do you know for sure?"

"TERN's physicists say so," Fabian said mildly. "I'll take their word for it."

Minh's blood pressure was still in the red. She dialed herself down, and a cool breeze washed over her as the blood drained from her skin.

Shit, she whispered to Kiki. *I promised myself I wouldn't argue with him. Why didn't you stop me?*

It was fun to watch. But you didn't really let go. You gave the banker worse.

They stepped out of the corridor onto a ledge overlooking a vast cavern. Below, a battery of machinery and status panels clung to a gleaming metal tube that disappeared into dark tunnels on either side.

"This is Launch and Retrieval," said Fabian. "The components visible here are a standard particle-accelerator array. TERN's proprietary technology is on the other side of the curve." He made a circle with his thumb and forefinger and tapped a knuckle. "Thirty kilometers away. That's where the physicists work."

Okay, this is impressive, Minh whispered to Kiki. *Even I'll admit it.*

The cavern was crowded with people—so many that the porters and loaders were crawling to their destinations at only a few meters per minute. And scattered across the wide floor were antiquities. Minh pinged them and brought their visuals into close-up.

Some were manikins draped with clothes from ancient cultures—wool and silk, every fiber harvested, dyed, spun, woven, cut, sewn, and embellished by hand. The human hours dedicated to their production were unimaginable. Some were religious icons, the wood more precious than the gold and silver. The metals might have been mass-produced from casts, but the wood was carved and painted by hand.

Minh especially liked the grotesque wooden saint's head, the top of its skull formed from glass displaying pieces of brown skull housed within. But best of all was the Minoan rhyton, a rock crystal vase laboriously reconstructed in the twentieth century from smashed fragments. Beside it was a second rhyton, identical but new and whole, direct from the artisan's workbench.

"Today is especially busy because we're processing a series of six-hour day trips," said Fabian. "Dhaka 1971, Victorian London, Heian Kyoto, the Ganga ghats. These are the shortest trips we offer. The waiting list is in the millions."

TERN staff in coveralls and boots wrangled groups of tourists. The crowd was dotted with people in historical costume—gowns, suits, hats, robes, wraps, and wigs. Tourists clustered around them.

"The people in costume are all strategic historians," Fabian said. "It's a glamour job. The ones dressed like me are tactical." Fabian nudged Hamid's elbow. "You're not wrong. Strategic and tactical do get in the occasional fight. And when they do, the best view is from right here."

10

AFTER THE SWANS AND monsters, Shulgi's falconers brought more disturbing reports. Red-eyed silver stones were spotted in every corner of the kingdom, floating high and low and dodging every missile thrown or launched at them. Fat, wingless hornets, too, by the thousands, comparatively easy to catch. When cut or squashed, they spilled clear liquid and shriveled to a speck.

In the moon temple, Susa spent another day arguing for Shulgi's death, then lost interest in her campaign. She receded into prayer and contemplation.

To Shulgi, Susa's retreat was the most disturbing portent of all.

~

From the vantage point of the ledge, Minh and her team watched as the tourists and historians were sealed into individual life-support sarcophaguses, stacked into carbon-fiber wireframes, and loaded into the curve. When they left, Launch and Retrieval was deserted except for a few techs and a dozen hygiene bots.

Fabian led them down into the main cavern and showed them their dedicated staging area. While Kiki and Hamid inventoried the equipment, Minh explored the accelerator array and its humming supplemental apparatus. A hygiene bot whirred across the floor, leaving a polished streak in its wake.

A tech with a nest of messy brown hair padded up to the edge of the accelerator tube and examined a clutch of bots as they whirred over its shining surface. When the bots disappeared into the tunnel, he lurked at the tunnel's entrance and sent a pair of cameras floating after them.

Minh stroked the side of the tube. It quivered under her suckers. A hum sounded from deep within the structure. She tapped the side of the tube.

"Can I climb on this?" she asked the tech. He looked tired, the skin under his eyes puffy and dark.

"Go ahead," he said. "The curve was built to last."

She snaked her legs up the side of the tube and dangled, belly against the cold metal, bracing herself with her hands. Once on top, she walked along a path of yellow safety treads bordered by grab bars. The treads were freshly painted, still slightly tacky under her toes.

Fabian wheeled an access ladder over, climbed up, and fell into step beside her.

"Do you have any questions about the project protocol?" he asked.

She gave him an acid look. "Didn't I pass my comprehension exams?"

He winced. "Let it go, Minh."

Are you fighting again? Do you need me to rescue you? Kiki whispered.

No, everything's professional. Lurk if you want.

"What are you concerned about, Fabian?"

He fired up the high-level work plan and the project setup workflows bloomed in the air.

"We won't have power when we land. But you can stay in your sarcophagus until the satellites begin providing ambient power."

"No, I'm not going to hide."

"When was the last time your legs were depowered?"

She scowled. "TERN's medical department can give you the details of every depowering over the last thirty years. You can also get a chart of my bowel movements, if you want."

Professional, Kiki whispered. *Why are you baiting him?*

It was a joke.

He didn't laugh.

If Fabian doesn't have a sense of humor, it's not my fault.

"I need to know how you're going to react when your legs yanked are out from under you," he said.

"Did you ask Kiki the same question?"

"I'm not worried about Kiki. She's easygoing. But you have a short fuse, and every time I try to handle you, you blow up. Are all plague babies like that? If so, life in the habs must be pretty ugly."

Kiki laughed. Minh had to struggle to keep from laughing along with her.

"I take it you're not worried about being without power," said Fabian.

Minh pinned him with a level, unblinking stare.

"Okay. You win." He put up his hands in mock surrender.

Give him a chance, Minh. He's only trying to do his job.

Maybe he could figure out how to do it without getting up my nose.

Fabian fell silent. He paced along beside her, seemingly lost in thought.

"I have a lot of respect for the habs and the work you do," he said when they reached the end of the curve. "When this project came up, I did a little research. I never understood the role of rivers on the surface of the planet before. They're like the human circulatory system."

"Not quite, but it's a useful metaphor," Minh said. "Rivers are the easy part of my work. Water flows downhill. Everything else is hard, and the worst part is getting people to work together."

"People are the hardest part of my job, too," he said. "So, can you do it?"

"Do what? Restore the Tigris and the Euphrates?" She chewed her lip. "Maybe, eventually. The habs have the people, the tech, and the experience, plus whole cohorts of fat babies itching for specialist training and real jobs. We'd love to put them to work."

"I know a little of your history. The habs were planning on population growth from immigration. When it didn't happen, you created the crèches."

"We were optimistic. We forgot most humans don't think on the long-term scale, and bankers certainly don't. They live in a fantasyland. But the habs were doing okay until ten years ago, when all of a sudden everyone decided TERN could magic all the world's problems away."

Stop baiting him, Kiki whispered. *He's trying to make friends.*

"You're not going to believe this," Fabian said, "but banker fantasies are a problem for TERN, too."

"They're a problem for the whole world."

He nodded. "When CEERD created TERN, they wanted to fix problems in the present by rewriting the past. For an economist, hindsight is a powerful tool. The world economic collapse, the extinction events, all the plagues and wars could be avoided if the right fix was applied at the right time, and we'd come out the other end with a healthy economic system and an intact population."

"With CEERD in charge, I suppose?"

Fabian stuffed his hands in his pockets. "CEERD had us doing backflips trying to find ways to force changes through the temporal barrier. Then they lost faith and cut their losses. Opened us up to commercial use."

"That's why you focus on tourism?"

He nodded. "You've probably noticed our hell is barebones. No luxuries, no aesthetics. We don't waste resources, because when we want to run our own time travel research projects or upgrade our equipment, we have to pay for it. CEERD won't float us anymore. They're strangling us with our internal trade deficit."

Fabian reached down and banged on the curve with his fist.

"Luckily, the tech is solid. And we know there's so much more we can do with it than taking tourists to ogle people in different clothes."

"Like Mesopotamian past-state assessments."

"We're historians. We love history. But you know what else gets us excited?"

Minh shrugged.

"Doing important work," he said. "Same as you. And what's more important than restoring ecosystems on the surface of the planet?"

Minh's eyebrows rose, surprised. "CEERD has never been interested in the habs."

"TERN isn't CEERD. We want out from under their thumb. Maybe this is the way."

"I don't like TERN," Minh said.

You're such a tough customer, Minh, Kiki whispered.

"But I want to work with you," Minh continued. "If our project proves out, every restoration project could begin with a past-state assessment. It would mean more robust restorations, and it would definitely shorten project timelines. Quicker completion means we could do more projects."

"Cheaper projects get funded," Fabian said.

"No, profitable projects get funded," she corrected. "And more human habitat means more people, and more people means more profit. I've spent enough time arguing with bankers to know what gets them panting."

"So have I. My father's an economic theorist, but he's a banker at heart. Nothing makes him happier than a column of numbers."

"Does he ever admit they're completely imaginary?"

"Never. Not in a million years."

"Bankers," Minh said, and they exchanged a smile.

11

SHULGI'S SPIES SAID THE moon temple was thrown into turmoil by Susa's change in behavior. Usually energetic and exacting, she'd receded into herself—talking to god, she claimed, though she never said which god. When she emerged from her prayers, she made bizarre demands.

She ordered the temple evacuated for an entire day, windows unshuttered, rooms and courtyards emptied of people and left for the wind to blow through. The surrounding streets milled with confused weavers, displaced potters, frightened pledges, angry managers, horrified cooks. Kilns full of vessels were ruined, vats of cloth corroded and stained, ovens cold, altars abandoned, gardens dry, lamps empty. Susa gave no explanation.

Over the next few days, she ordered her people to blindfold themselves and recite every song, story, prayer, and fable they knew—not only in the language of the temples but in every tongue.

Susa had gone mad.

~

TERN's project protocol simulations hadn't prepared Minh for landing in 2024 BCE. Swaddled in a felt coverall, her face layered with a thick gel mask, she expected to feel trapped, even stifled. Instead she felt naked, flayed. Her eyes were glued shut with mucus. Her muscles shivered. Her skin stung as if stretched.

Joints creaking, Minh pulled herself over the edge of her sarcophagus. Her legs were locked protectively against her crotch, six coils stiff as fists against the soft flesh. She slipped her hands out of her sleeves and felt her neck. The goiter clung like a leech, twitching. Her diaphragm cycled inert gas from the mask's bubble mouthpiece to her lungs while the goiter fed oxygen into her trachea and flushed carbon dioxide from her blood. The mask's noise-canceling tech buzzed white noise in her ears.

She pulled at the goiter. It detached from her throat and hung, swinging against her collarbone by the last few strands buried in her neck.

Minh eased her fingernails under the edges of the mask and pried it away from her temples. The side pieces released first, sliding out of her ears with a slurp. A faint breeze caressed her wet skin. More white noise now, ocean surf and wind.

Using her fingernails, she tried to pry the mask from under her chin, but it barely lifted. She stuck out her tongue to force the gel away from her lips. The piece snaking down her gullet gave slightly—enough to trigger her gag reflex. Bile prickled her throat.

Minh wanted to launch the first satellite. The mask would peel off in a minute or two and then she'd be able to see, but she wasn't going to wait.

She felt around until her fingertips brushed the satellite launcher case. She flipped the safety catches and pulled the arming tabs. They gave way with satisfying pops, and the ignition primed with a faint buzz. She pulled the launcher close to her chest, tucked the barrel behind her ear, and clicked the triggers.

It didn't fire. Something overhead was blocking the sights. Likely a tree. She needed a better position.

Minh slid out of the sarcophagus, flopping onto her belly. Cool sand cradled her torso. She wiggled, dragging the launcher behind her with one hand. Then she dug the butt of the housing in the sand, braced it between her elbow and gut, and hit the triggers again.

Warmth bloomed against her stomach. The launcher buzzed and heaved.

The mask peeled from her eyelids. She convulsed—violent, lung-bruising coughs. The mask peeled out of her throat and plopped between her elbows. Eyelashes were embedded in eye sockets. The goiter landed beside it, wiggling. She raked sand over it with the blade of her hand.

The air smelled like biofiltration mats from the bowels of Calgary's water recirculation system, with a whiff of something rotten, like a dirty extruder nozzle, so oxygen-thick it seemed like the air might catch fire from any spark.

Fabian bent over his sarcophagus, his face red and blotched.

"Who got the first satellite up?" he asked. "Bet it was Minh."

"Of course it was Minh," said Hamid. He staggered over to Kiki's sarcophagus, flipped it open, and reached in with both arms.

"I'm okay." Kiki's voice was muffled. "Really dizzy, though. I don't know which way is up. And this thing is still wiggling."

Kiki's hand appeared. She flipped her goiter into the air. When it rolled to Fabian's feet, he kicked sand over it.

"Are you going to get number two and three up, Minh?" he asked.

"Already on it." Minh slammed a new cartridge into the launcher and dug its butt into the sand.

"When you're done, give it a rest. You've just time traveled. Stop trying to do it all and enjoy the view."

She primed the ignition, braced the barrel, and thumbed the triggers again. The launcher's tip glowed orange and burped a fist-sized ball of fire into the sky. Minh watched it fade and disappear overhead. Then she repeated the process with a third satellite.

"Ambient power in ninety minutes," Fabian said. "LAN in a hundred. Drink some water. You can launch the rest of the satellites in a minute."

He pushed a bottle into her hand. She guzzled it. Then, finally, she looked around.

Cobalt ocean and pale beach curved in a lazy arc toward rocky headlands. White rollers licked the shore. Pink clouds scudded across the horizon, and a faint green band marked the point where sky kissed water. Behind her, slender palm trees arced over the black carbon-fiber wireframe encasing their equipment. Gears on mechanical timers had released the sarcophaguses onto the sand like swollen petals.

"Welcome to Home Beach." Fabian scanned the horizon with a pair of binoculars. "This is where we begin every new baseline. We're in the remote South Pacific. No settlements within a thousand kilometers, but I'm checking to be sure. Past population members do tend to wander."

He lowered the binoculars and cast a worried glance at Kiki's sarcophagus. The only part of Kiki visible was her fist gripping Hamid's hand.

"How you doing in there, Kiki?" Fabian asked.

"Good now. Hamid gave me an anti-nauseant." She sat up and looked around. "Wow, this is gorgeous."

"I'm going to check the other side of the island," Fabian said. "Stay out of the water. The jellyfish are deadly."

"This is weird," Kiki said. "No stream, no whispers, no message queue, nothing to ping. I'm used to juggling a dozen feeds and conversations, but now I can't even see my biom." She thrust her arms out in a wide circle. "And no people. We're alone."

"If we want to gossip about each other, we'll have to do it the old-fashioned way," Hamid said.

He took Kiki's wrist between his fingers and counted her pulse, beating his foot on the sand to judge the rhythm. When a huge bird splashed across the water not a hundred meters offshore, he dropped her hand and jumped to his feet.

"A frigatebird," he said. "Where's Fabian? I need those binoculars."

Minh dragged herself over to the wireframe and heaved a lever. A storage compartment slid open. She dug out a slender telescope and flipped it to Hamid.

He lifted the scope and tracked the bird as it circled the beach.

"A frigatebird," he repeated. "Wow. I'm never going home."

~

Hamid identified five more bird species before ambient power hit. Minh's biom bloomed in the bottom left of her eye—all green, no alerts. Her legs unfurled, and the instant she was mobile, she scooted down to the shore to dangle a toe in the warm water. Thumb-sized jellyfish clustered in the shallows, their threadlike tentacles translucent against the creamy sand, their bodies and arms a delicate apricot. Kiki skipped down the beach to join Minh and then ran along the water's edge, laughing, leaving a trail of chevron-shaped hoofprints in the wet sand.

When the LAN came up, Minh's feeds and bookmarks stacked into their usual positions on the bottom right of her visual field. Minh booted a seer and put it on the upper left. It began identifying species right away. Minh dismissed the taxonomy and set the interface to supply the most relevant indigenous names. The palm trees were thangithake, mostly, with a few unidentified species. She'd take a closer look later.

She grabbed a camera and sent it spinning overhead. From a ten-meter elevation she could survey the whole island. Home Beach was the right size for a three-week ecological assessment. A hundred thousand square kilometers was ridiculous. The sheer enormity of the project loomed overhead. What had she been thinking? This was going to be a disaster.

Minh took a deep breath. She always got vertigo at the start of every big project. It would all work out fine. One task at a time.

"Satellites are streaming," Fabian called out. He fired the feed across the horizon.

Home Beach was at the far eastern edge of a widespread archipelago. The feed was dotted with population markers and estimates of human biomass, but nothing within five hundred kilometers. Markers tracked a flotilla all alone in the wide ocean, far from land.

Kiki zoomed in. People were clustered in the open boats like seeds in tiny pods. She magnified the feed until the people were fuzzy splotches.

"I wish we could see their faces," Kiki said.

Minh collapsed the feed and replaced it with the day's work breakdown.

"It's time to start ticking boxes," she said.

While Kiki fabbed construction elements, Minh and Hamid assembled their pocket hab—a temporary dome with sleep cubbies, nutrition, and hygiene support. Fabian began assembling the skip and its pad. Floats did the heavy work, shuttling components from the wire-frame and moving newly fabbed pieces to the assembly sites.

Kiki hadn't exaggerated her fabbing skills; she knew how to optimize the output and keep the tech from choking. When Minh lurked on Kiki's feed, the spinning workflows looked nearly as complex as a climate stats array. Kiki was watching the satellite feed, too, zooming in on villages as she monitored the fab.

The pocket hab was basic, a tiny, two-level dome with a negative-pressure system to keep the bugs out. Furniture was minimal—benches around a communal table downstairs, and four sleep cubbies above.

Kiki had added a green leaf pattern to the dome's skin, echoing the shades and shape of the thangithake palms. Viewed from the beach, the hab blended into the landscape. It was an illusion, though. Their footprint was already on the ecosystem, heavier than Minh liked. Water recirculation took gray water from shower to toilet, and sewage went straight into a tank with no treatment, just a hose to exhaust the gas away from camp. Their routes between fab, hab, skip, and beach were already cutting through the ground cover. Minh was keeping an eye on a purarata growing near one of the trails, not for the shrub itself, though its deep red flower and elongated pistils were impressive, but for the unidentifiable clusters of mold growing on its stalk. She'd have to take a sample home, for curiosity's sake.

Minh prepped the maintenance bot while Hamid assembled the nutritional extruder and bolted it to the table. As lunch was priming, he unpacked a carton of floating cameras, waking them one by one and letting them float into the air from his palm. Then he filled his bowl and trotted down to the shore, cameras following behind.

Fabian sent the skip on its test burn and joined Minh and Kiki in the hab. They watched the egg-shaped amber skip slowly follow its invisible power beam and disappear into the sky.

"How do you keep tourists occupied during setup?" Kiki asked as she scooped lunch into her bowl. "They'd get bored with all this fabbing and start wandering off."

"We keep tourists under wraps until everything's ready," Fabian said. "On day trips, we only support nutrition and hygiene. Since we're always dropping into the same baseline, we don't have to worry about surprises from weather or past populations. We've seen it all before."

"Today is new, though." Kiki was half-buried in the local satellite feed, tracking population markers, zooming in on a large island village where individuals moved like ants across the beach. "New to you, I mean. You've never lived through today before."

He smiled patiently. "I haven't lived through it yet. Anything could happen. This is uncharted territory."

"It's getting less uncharted all the time," Minh said.

She copied Kiki's feed and collapsed it to a globe. Half the planet was dark, the poles were grayed out, and large weather systems blotted the sphere with milky pinwheels, but most of the satellites were in position, lighting up the continents with data.

Dawn crept across Asia. Minh zoomed in on the Yangtze River, its vast braided delta and wide course lit with a rosy glow. She could easily immerse herself in the rivers of the world, but she didn't have to do it now. The satellite feeds were downloading to the information core. Nothing trapped would get lost, and she had other responsibilities.

On the other side of the world, it was midnight over Mesopotamia. The satellites there—the most powerful ones—were only beginning to extend their sensing arrays. In another six hours, they would be fully operational, and the Tigris and Euphrates would reveal themselves.

Minh slapped down the feed and shot the workflow onto the table.

"The shelter is fabbed and the satellites are all in place," she said. "Our first landing in Mesopotamia isn't on the schedule for two more days, but I want to move it up. Kiki can fab the sampling equipment next."

Kiki nodded, her mouth full.

"When does the skip get back?" Minh asked Fabian.

He fired the skip feed onto the table. The dashboard indicators were all green.

"Five hours. Looks like the fuselage is curing properly so far."

Kiki scraped the last spoonful out of her bowl and then set it on the floor in front of the hygiene bot.

"Where are you sending it?" she asked.

Fabian raised a finger as he finished chewing. He swallowed and said, "I always send my test burns to Stonehenge. Bring it right down in the middle."

Kiki stared. "What about the people there?"

"They get out of the way."

Fabian picked a bit of congealed protein out of his bowl.

"That's not right," Kiki said. "You can't do that."

Two tiny furrows appeared between Kiki's eyebrows. She looked to Minh for support.

"I assume it's part of TERN's health and safety protocol," Minh said. "Hitting a hard target tests the guidance system."

"No," Fabian said. "Stonehenge is my own choice."

"Why? It's cruel," said Kiki.

Fabian tapped his spoon on the table, clearly irritated.

"Cruel? They practice human sacrifice. Want to see the docs?"

Kiki glared at him. "Reroute the skip. You can't terrorize people for fun."

"What if they attack the skip?" Minh asked. "They could damage it."

Fabian shrugged. "If the skip can't handle Bronze Age weapons, we shouldn't be flying in it." He balled his fists on the table. "Did you fab the skip fuselage correctly?"

Kiki's shoulders climbed up to her ears. "Of course. I'm an experienced tech."

"Would you fly in it without testing?"

"No, that would be stupid. But you can cure and stress-test the fuselage without terrifying people."

Fabian pointed his spoon at her. "Health and safety is my responsibility. I know how to do my job."

Kiki turned her attention back to the feed, where tiny blots of people were going about their days.

"Fine," she said. "Just don't try it with these people."

-12-

SUSA'S PEOPLE RANGED THROUGH the kingdom, gathering insects and worms and closing them into containers. Then, Susa seized land. With no explanation, she canceled the leases on a wide strip of fields between two arms of the river and cleared everyone off it, leaving the crops to wave in the wind untended. Susa stacked the land with tribute—that was the only word for it. An array of temple furnishings, mirrors, caskets, and gems, all gathered inside her own traveling tent.

Susa's instructions were clear. No one was allowed to visit those fields without her permission. But Shulgi was king. He didn't have to ask permission of anyone but the gods.

He called in his falconers and brought them to council among his wives in one of the palace's lowest and darkest storerooms. The falconers all agreed: They were being watched—everyone was being watched. Not only by the red-eyed silver things and the hollow hornets but by unseen creatures from above. Perhaps by the new stars themselves.

Shulgi believed his falconers. It took a watcher to recognize another watcher.

Against an unknown enemy, only one strategy would succeed: stealth.

~

When the main satellites began posting tomography and topography data, Minh glued herself to the feed. On the other side of the globe, Mesopotamia was still dark; true-color remote sensing would have to wait for daylight. The rivers came up in wireframe first as the geographical survey began a preliminary pass. When the details started filling in, she drilled deep into the data, spreading the terrain around her until she could hang right over the narrowest point of the interfluve.

She anchored her view to an imaginary point a hundred meters above the ground, where she could see both rivers on either side. Below, the tomography registered a mud brick city in three-dimensional detail, cubes hardly less dense than the surrounding terrain, the geography distorted by roads, paddocks, shacks, fences, paths, berms, walls, pits—an unending array of meaningless complications. A tangle of human-made data anomalies messing up her geophysical overview.

When she excluded right angles from the synthesis,

most of the anomalies flattened out. Now she could see the landscape in its pure form, with no human interference. No sound, no color, no texture detail, but the two rivers were within her grasp.

Minh lifted her perspective to a thousand meters, two thousand. Now the whole trench spread below her. The Tigris and Euphrates in full spring flow, fed generously at their sources with freshet from the snow-covered mountains to the north, and further swollen by tributaries snaking down from the surrounding highlands. Their channels braided the plain, pulling away from the main lobe formed millennia in the past, its paleochannel buried deep in the geological strata, and now forming new lobes—the complex web of a mature river system.

The Tigris was the newest major channel. Since splitting away from the Euphrates hundreds of years in the past, the Tigris now rushed to the ocean, depositing its suspended sediment to rapidly infill the shallow upper gulf and form a new wide delta, stranding the old salt marsh far from shore.

The data gushing in made Minh dizzy. She couldn't keep up with it. The river channels were complex enough, but they were further complicated by human intervention—canals, drainage ditches, irrigation channels, dikes, spoil banks, mill ponds, stewponds, wells, dams—flow diversions of every kind. These complications were important, too. When humans tried to control water, they did so for a reason.

So much data, and this was only the first pass.

To control the rising panic, she pulled back to what she knew. Pushed her perspective north to the mountains, to the main channel and tributary sources, where the water flowed cold, clear, and fast.

Minh had spent her life working with high mountain rivers—steep channels with turbulent courses. She was used to managing flows using precise climatic, groundwater, and snowpack accounting, drawing on moment-to-moment microclimate reporting confirmed with batteries of floating microgauges. The rivers she studied were modeled and monitored—every channel, reach, meander, seam, eddy, and boil. Carefully managed rivers that never reached the ocean, that surrendered their flow over to the habs for use and reuse, treated and recirculated again and again until eventually, inevitably escaping to atmosphere.

But she still hadn't actually seen the Tigris and Euphrates yet. Not with her own eyes. The true color image was lit only by moonlight, ashy rivers in a charcoal landscape. But it wouldn't be long now.

When the sun came up over west Asia, the terrain slowly came to light. At last, as the sun drew back the mountains' shadow, she saw them, their wide channels like veins splitting the emerald fields, bleeding cloudy brown into the sapphire gulf. The sight stole her breath away.

"I didn't expect the rivers to be polluted," Fabian said.

He stood at Minh's shoulder, lurking on her feed, his bare toes dug into the same patch of beach sand she was gently stirring with her legs.

"I've seen the rivers several times before, in different ages," he explained. "I assumed the water was clean until I saw this." He pointed at the effluent.

It was a stupid comment, but Fabian was no more ignorant than her old Tuk-U students. Minh could afford to be patient.

"This water isn't polluted, it's loaded with nutrient-rich sediment. The floods deposit the sediment, making the soil highly productive and allowing the geography to support a large population. We don't know how large yet, but we will soon."

Minh killed the right-angle smoothing, and the buildings popped back into the feed. She lifted the perspective to encompass the whole project area, and then added the population layer.

The population numbers surprised her. Quarter of a million and climbing as the biological load was recalculated and revised.

"These numbers must be wrong," she said.

"The estimate will get a lot higher," he said. "Are you sure those rivers aren't polluted?"

A chill ran down Minh's spine. With such a huge population, they must be.

"I'd have to sample to be sure."

"Past population members dump everything into the rivers, you know. Sewage, corpses, effluent from tanning and dyeing. Those industries are toxic."

Minh didn't answer. She didn't want to know.

Fabian applied an overlay from TERN's datastore, labeling cities across the trench. Many villages and cities popped up question marks.

Fabian centered the feed on a city on the Euphrates' alluvial fan. He shift-tilted the feed to show the city at a less extreme angle, as if from an imaginary mountaintop to the north.

"This is Ur," he said. "In this era, political power is centered here."

A huge city surrounded by a thick earthen wall. And crowded with people. More poured out of the houses onto the lanes and squares every moment. Crowded with animals, too. Horses, camels, donkeys, mules, cows, goats, pigs, sheep. Domestic livestock of every kind, and birds in pens, cages, tied to perches, and flying wild.

Is Hamid seeing this? she asked Kiki.

Yeah, he's disintegrating, Kiki replied. *Are you with*

Fabian? Don't kill each other, okay?

Fabian panned across the city, zooming in on a street where carcasses lay piled, a tannery where skins buzzed with flies, and an industrial clearing where hooves and bones boiled in vats. Then he zoomed in on a massive complex at the city center.

In contrast to the dun-colored lesser buildings on the outskirts, the city center was packed with huge, multilevel structures, brightly colored and patterned, with leafy court-yards. Temples and palaces, she guessed. They circled a multilevel ziggurat. Its pyramid form was carved into ter-races, planted with greenery, studded with statues, and pit-ted with alcoves. Staircases ascended each level on all four sides, and people clustered on every level. The apex was crowded, too. The people there were performing a cere-mony, passing a golden bowl back and forth.

They were all young and obsessively overgroomed, with complex braided and curled hairstyles and intricate makeup, dripping with gold jewelry and gems. Despite the festival atmosphere their dress implied, they all looked anxious, glancing at the sky as if expecting a bolt of lightning. The young man at the center of the cere-mony was naked except for his jewelry, every plane and curve of his physique emphasized by body paint. His gold cap was so heavy, it pressed his eyebrows into a per-manent frown.

"That's Shulgi," said Fabian. "King of Ur. This is the first time anyone's ever seen him."

The short woman at Shulgi's shoulder was furious, her smooth young face contorting as she spat out her prayers. When it was her turn to pass the golden bowl to Shulgi, she shoved it at him so suddenly, he nearly dropped it.

"You're losing a lot of data here, aren't you? Without sound, you'll never know what they're so upset about." Minh asked.

Fabian shrugged. "I'll drop the bugs when we land."

Minh watched the short woman fume at the king for another minute, but it didn't look like the ceremony was ending anytime soon. When Minh abandoned Fabian's feed to go back to her own work, she expected him to wander off, but he dropped it, too, and tagged along with hers. She fired up the population estimate dashboard.

"Are these numbers accurate?"

Fabian nodded. "In this climate, past population members are active in the cool morning, but they retreat inside during the hottest—"

She interrupted him. "I want to do the first landing tomorrow. Soil mapping is a big job. If we start early, we might be able to squeeze in an extra landing at the end of the project."

"Okay," he said. "Your team has a lot of work to do before then."

"No problem. Now listen. I honestly didn't expect such a large population. How easily will we be able to move around?"

"You can't go far. On the first landing, we'll have time to put the evac gurneys and sampling equipment into place, not much more than that. Ten minutes, more or less."

"I can take soil samples in ten minutes," she said. "But people are everywhere. Is that going to be a problem? Our landing sites have to support our project goals. We can't just choose sites based on safety."

"Give me your wish list and I'll find a way to make it happen."

Fabian left her alone then, and Minh immersed herself in her work.

When the sun set over the south Pacific, Minh laid her feed over inky ocean and sky spangled with southern hemisphere constellations. Three local satellites winked overhead. Behind her, moths fluttered around the pocket hab's lights. Inside, Hamid and Kiki were refining the biological sampling plan, checking boxes on the work breakdown. Good.

Minh worked through the Mesopotamian day until the sun set over her rivers. Then, as a brief dawn rose over the beach, she retreated to the hab and joined Hamid and Kiki at the table.

"Show me the horses," Minh told Hamid. "I know you. First thing you looked for."

He yawned and fired a stack of bookmarks onto the table.

Minh flipped through them. "Looks like there might be a few horses in Mesopotamia."

"A couple of rivers, too," he replied. They shared a gleeful grin.

"You should have seen him dancing around when the sun rose," Kiki said. "I was going to shoot you the feed, but you were busy having your moment with the rivers."

None of them could stop yawning once Hamid got them going. When they dragged themselves to bed, Fabian was getting up. His bare feet dangled from his cubby.

"We're ready to land," said Minh. "Three potential sites are waiting in your queue."

He yawned. "I'll work out the details while you sleep."

I lurked on your feed a few times, Kiki whispered as Minh settled into her sleep stack. *You were in wireframe mostly. Did you take any time out to look at the people?*

Fabian showed me a ceremony on a ziggurat. The people looked grumpy.

Hamid and I saw the ceremony, too. You missed the animal sacrifices.

What did Hamid think about those?

He didn't like it, but he got a lot of data. It was like they'd brought out all their best stock for him to tag and catalogue.

What did you think? Did it bother you?

A pause. Minh thought Kiki had drifted off to sleep. Then she answered.

You're always expecting me to make trouble, aren't you? But I've never given you any reason. Is there anyone you trust?

I just want to know what you thought.

I think the people are on edge because of the satellites. New stars in the sky—of course they'd notice. And they must think it means something.

Good observation.

I never expected the people here to act like us. But I didn't expect them to be so young. It's weird to see people my age in charge.

Population dynamics are different here.

Young, old, it doesn't matter. I liked seeing their faces.

SHULGI PICKED HIS FIVE strongest swimmers. They'd used an underwater approach before, to make forays into hostile territory and execute sneak attacks, but never at night.

The six of them moved through the river, naked, swimming to within striking position and then waiting in the river for dawn. The monster was watching for them, but instead of attacking, it retreated to its egg. They hit the egg with nets and arrows. The attack had no effect at first. The egg rose high, but then it began to fall.

Shulgi caught a horse and galloped after the amber egg as it arced through the sky and skipped across the earth, throwing dirt behind it like a cock's tail.

∼

The first landing began with full stomachs. Fabian netted fish, grilled them over an open fire, flaked the flesh, and mixed it with extruded protein, starch, coconut, and a packet of spices. Kedgeree, he called it.

They ate on the beach under the slanting evening light. Hamid and Kiki kicked sand at each other and giggled like a couple of crechies. When Fabian passed Minh a mug of tea and said he'd approved her first choice of landing spot, she nearly hugged him.

The cozy, convivial atmosphere evaporated when Fabian began lecturing them.

"I know you're eager to get working," he said. "But I want to go over the project protocol."

Minh sighed and refilled her mug.

"Before you start complaining, Minh, wait. I'm going to tell you three things you don't already know. First, the landing is going to go by really quickly. When we're skipping out, you'll feel disappointed. You traveled four thousand years just to spend ten minutes messing with equipment in a field somewhere. That's okay. We'll have more time on the next landing.

"Second, you should know we don't even need to leave the skip. We can drop off the evac gurneys, throw the cameras and monitors out the door, turn around, and run the whole project from Home Beach. You could go back to Calgary with a nice tan."

"But—" said Kiki.

Minh interrupted her. "We can do a lot with remote sensing, but those results need to be ground-truthed with manual sampling."

"I know," said Fabian. "You didn't come here to sit on a beach. You want to see the project site with your own eyes. That means you've already accepted a certain level of risk."

He unzipped his coverall and pulled down the collar of his undershirt. A palm-sized lump of scar tissue webbed the flesh under his collarbone.

"I got this in Jerusalem, on my third trip. It was an arrow. I knew past population members killed people with sticks and stones, but it was hot. I had my hood down and my coverall unzipped. I felt invincible."

"Why didn't you have the scar tissue removed?" Kiki asked.

"It's a teaching tool. I use it to remind people that coveralls can't protect uncovered skin and, in any case, will only protect against piercing and slashing. They do very little against blunt-force trauma."

"We'll keep our coveralls zipped and our hoods up," said Minh.

"At least until the situation is under control," said Fabian.

Hamid gave Fabian a narrow, assessing glance. "That's not why you kept the scar."

"Hamid the large mammal specialist has me all figured out," Fabian said. "Okay, why?"

"It separates you from the strategic historians. I bet

everyone in tactical has an impressive scar. In fact, I bet you're not considered a real tactical historian until you have one."

"That would be barbaric." Fabian chewed on the inside of his cheek, considering it. "But you're not far wrong."

"What's the third thing?" asked Minh. "I want to start classifying microclimates."

"The third thing is, I want to thank you for being adventurous. For trusting me to keep you safe. I'll do everything I can to get you back to Home Beach today, and back to Calgary when the project is complete. I have a perfect safety record. It's not going to change."

When the meal was over, they tossed their dishes to the bot, changed into their protective coveralls, and loaded their equipment.

It was the smallest skip Minh had ever seen. Four seats, equipment in the cargo pit under their feet, and sleek safety-foam canisters overhead. Fabian offered Minh and Hamid the front seats. Fabian sat behind Minh, and Kiki strapped in behind Hamid.

On the inside of the fuselage, Kiki had fabbed a decorative relief of peaches.

The skip needs a name. Lucky Peach, Kiki whispered. *I thought you might be getting homesick for your orchard.*

On the upskip, Minh worked on her climate data, but once over land, she found herself staring at the skip's feed. Their great circle route kissed the islands of southern Japan, shot across China, and skirted vast mountain ranges of central Asia. Their downskip initiated south of the Caspian Sea, a slow, controlled hurtle to earth.

At a thousand meters' elevation, they raked through a flock of migrating birds. Their bodies thudded against the skip. Minh dug her nails into the foam restraints. Hamid shuddered.

"Whooper swans," he said.

"The skip is fine," Fabian said. "This design is rated for far bigger in-air collisions."

"Birds don't get much bigger than that."

"They do in the Cretaceous."

They descended over a field near a side channel of the Euphrates, at the far west side of the trench. The location offered a robust cross-section of land use—grazing, fields, orchards—but Minh only cared about the river. The reach was shallow and, unlike the main channel, appeared to have suffered only minimal human disturbance. Fruit trees studded the field, and green crops hugged the irrigated zone along the outer edge of the bend, sandwiched between the river and a steep rocky upland covered with carob, terebinth, and olive.

Fabian fired an infrared feed onto the forward bulkhead. "I've tagged and categorized past population members within three square kilometers. There are nearly two hundred, mostly agricultural laborers. Nine are nearby. They're tired—they've been working all morning, and now they're resting under the trees. I don't think they'll get too close."

Minh's patience was spent. Two and a half hours in a confined space with Fabian was enough.

"This is the health and safety workflow," she said. "It has nothing to do with us."

"Health and safety has everything to do with you."

"Not if you do your job right."

"Give me a minute. There's military all around. The camp at the top of the ridge will send down a patrol. We can also expect a response from the closest village, five kilometers downstream, and the town ten kilometers up-river. They'll come by boat, and they'll move fast."

"Are you done?" Minh asked.

"One final reminder," Fabian said. "When I give the word, retreat to the skip. Top speed."

Minh pulled up the skip's feed. They were a hundred meters above ground, descending slowly. The ground cover below was so green, it was nearly shocking. Her seer couldn't identify the type of grain yet. At the edge of the field, on the rocky ground near a wide carob tree, piles of crops smoked as if they were on fire. Figures popped out from under the carob canopy, each one tagged with a green diamond and an ID code. They stared up at the descending skip, brows contracted.

But those people were Fabian's problem, not hers.

Minh grabbed the live satellite feed and overlaid the geographical targets for her workflow. It was ridiculously simple: two sediment samples using grab samplers, six benthic samples using slack nets, and as many core and water samples as she could get.

When the skip touched down, her whole body hummed, eager to get outside.

Fabian split the hatch. Hot air blasted into the skip. It smelled of herbs and smoke—like the inside of a tandoori oven she'd once seen, in a restaurant in Cusco, when Byron was treating. The levels of oxygen nearly made her swoon.

"Cameras up," Fabian said.

A clutch of silver cameras flew out the hatch and circled the skip.

"Evac gurneys up."

Four large floats slid out of the cargo pit and rose slowly toward the sun.

Minh watched Fabian closely. He could call this off at any moment, seal the door and prep the upskip.

"Boots down," he said.

Minh was first out the door. She unshipped her cargo floats and ran through the field at top speed. The floats and one of Fabian's cameras tailed her.

Barley. Minh's seer identified the species. But not planted in neat rows, and not a monoculture. Forbs were scattered through the field. Planted, wild, or volunteer? But no time to stop.

Halfway to the river, the barley field turned sodden. The Euphrates had sprung its banks and licked its wet tongue into the field. Wherever the water touched, the crop was harvested, stiff shorn stalks poking from the mud. But why? The barley wasn't ripe yet. In the dry parts of the field, the stalks were green and flexible, spikes narrow and clenched.

Maybe she should have brought an agronomist.

Minh spun through the feeds. Fabian had a camera trained on the farmers. They stood in the shade near the smoking piles of grain, watching the strangers, their faces twisted with shock and fear. The burning crop was green barley. Salvaging the grain from the flood, she guessed.

Everything's fine, Fabian whispered. *The local past population members don't know what to do about us yet. They'll probably stay in the shade. And the military response hasn't even started. We have time.*

Minh hit one of her soil sample targets. She shot a corer into the mud, twisted off the sample cartridge, and laid it carefully on the float. She gathered five more cores as she made her way across the soggy field to an old fig tree on the riverbank. She sent her overhead camera ahead to trap the flood scars on its gnarled trunk.

My sampling nests are all moving out into position, whispered Hamid, *and the evac gurneys have released the biodiversity survey bots. Your gauges in the water yet?*

Minh laughed. *No, I'm still playing in the mud.*

She called the floats carrying the riverine survey cameras and gauges, sent it over the surface of the river, and tipped them all in. Then it was time to get wet.

Erosion exposed half the fig tree's root system. Long cords reached down the abraded bank, clutching the soil. She gripped the trunk with two of her legs and lowered herself into the river.

She couldn't stop grinning—she was made for this kind of work. Stretched out underwater, she held fast to the roots, shoved the grab sampler into the sediment, and hit the trigger. When the blade sliced cleanly through the sediment, Minh hauled the dripping muddy mass to the top of the bank.

She was breathing hard and shaking. Blood pressure shooting through the orange zone. She dialed her adrenaline response way down. Tension drained from her body. Her coveralls clung.

Can I get rid of these clothes, or are you still worried about health and safety? she asked Fabian.

I'm surprised you still have them on. I bet Hamid you'd be down to your undershirt five meters from the skip.

Minh rolled her eyes at the camera overhead. She flipped down her hood but left her coverall zipped. As she dragged a water sampling rack through the river, she took a moment to look in on her team. Hamid was checking boxes on the biodiversity survey as Kiki collected geology samples.

Minh ran forty meters upstream to her next sampling point—a willow thicket hunched around a granite outcropping. Mud slurped under her toes; flies buzzed around her head.

There's a two-kilo mammal ahead. Fabian whispered. *Don't be startled.*

A rabbit burst from under a willow and fled, splashing through the floodwater. Minh crawled into the thicket, plucked a tuft of fur from a thorny forb, and tucked it into a sampling envelope along with a few grains of feces.

Small boat coming downstream. Finish up and head back to the skip.

Fabian fired her a satellite bookmark tracking a slender boat with six people rowing furiously. The contact countdown showed seven and a half minutes.

One sediment sample, a half dozen cores, a few racks of water samples, and genetic material from a rabbit. Not nearly enough. But seven minutes was a long time. She wasn't worried.

Minh splashed into the river with the second grab

sampler. The water was deeper there—good—she wanted to get wet again. She snaked a leg into the sediment, found a submerged root, and pulled herself down to take the sample.

Sputtering, she broke surface and called the float over. The sample was ungainly—when she tried to lift it overhead, she nearly dropped it.

Kiki and I are packing up, Hamid whispered. *Send your float ahead so we can get your samples stowed.*

Four minutes left. She could get one more benthic sample on the way back to the skip. Maybe two.

Minh hooked her fingers around the edge of the float and sent it coasting downriver, back toward the fig tree. She held tight and floated behind it, legs trailing.

Minh, what are you doing? Kiki whispered. *Do you want to get killed?*

I told Kiki you wouldn't listen, Fabian whispered.

Minh shoved a slack net into the mud, then grabbed another net and shifted ten meters downstream.

They're soldiers. They have weapons, Kiki whispered. *Two minutes away. Can't you see the countdown?*

Minh bagged the samples and threw them onto the float.

Minh, get back here now, whispered Hamid.

She sent the float back to the skip and looked at the feed.

Six men rounded the bend, reaching hard with their paddles. The narrow boat was low in the water. Their faces gleamed with sweat. They were young, bare-chested, their shoulders covered in short cloaks. Their boat bristled with thick lances, long shining spines tipped with gleaming blades.

The contact counter flashed zero.

Same thing, every time, Fabian whispered. *Someone gets into trouble.*

Minh yanked herself out of the water and fled through the soaked barley field. Her legs churned the mud, ripping up plants by their roots.

You have eyes in the back of your head, Fabian whispered. *Use them.*

Minh checked her camera feed. The boat's prow bucked as it skidded up the inundated riverbank. Three soldiers leapt out, lances in hand. Chasing her—three men, now six.

She should be faster than any human on this terrain, but the soldiers were gaining on her. Close behind—only ten meters. Nine.

A shadow streaked toward them. A black drone coasted over the soldiers' heads. Its surface was studded with a sensor array.

The drone flashed. A soldier fell face-first in the mud. Another dropped beside him. The third fell to his knees and raised his lance, then teetered over backward. The remaining three skidded and ran for the cover of the fig tree. The drone chased them, flashed three times. They fell before they could reach cover.

The contact counter reset to six minutes.

Minh's momentum carried her all the way to the skip, but she wasn't watching where she was going. She was looking at the bodies lying in the wet field.

She collapsed against the side of the *Peach*, smearing mud over the amber fuselage. Kiki stood above her, framed by the skip's hatch, coverall sleeves tied around her waist. Her arms were muddy to the elbows. Behind her, Hamid clutched a box of samples.

"Why did you kill them?" Kiki glared at Fabian, teeth bared. Furious. "You didn't have to kill them."

My fault. I wasn't thinking, Minh whispered.

Fabian held out his hand. The drone skated through the air, retracted its sensory array, and settled on his palm.

"Calm down, Kiki," he said. "Everything's fine."

"It's not fine. They're dead," Kiki spat.

"Better them than Minh."

"You could have tried something else. Anything else."

"Next time," he said.

-14-

WHEN SHULGI REACHED THE fallen egg, people were converging on the site from the surrounding fields. He ordered them to leave the area, but they weren't eager to obey. He was a strange naked man bearing no marks of authority, attended by no retinue, wearing no regalia. But the horse and his weapons were enough to impress them. They didn't leave, but backed away to watch from a distance.

The monster scrambled backward through the mud and squeezed itself inside the egg. Six legs, yes; the barley farmers hadn't been mistaken. Perhaps two had been lost in battle. Was it a human turned half-octopus or an octopus turned half-person? Was its spirit half-beast, or just its body? And where were its companions?

When Shulgi's soldiers joined him, he would find out.

～

Through the whole flight back to Home Beach, Minh stuck close to the barley field feeds. Her camera orbited above the dead men, showing flies landing delicately on their ears, their lips, their staring eyes. Within a few minutes, a dozen soldiers arrived from a camp on the western ridge. When they spotted the bodies, they ran through the sodden field, gathered the dead in their arms, and wiped the mud from their blank faces. They hauled the corpses to the river, piled the carcasses on a barge, and floated them downstream.

Minh followed. But by the time they dropped into downskip over Home Beach, she'd seen enough. Every time someone looked into the eye of the camera overhead—into Minh's eye—she saw the same thing. Anger. Fear. Confusion. It was too much.

After they landed, Minh put her fake on duty, crawled into her cubby, and slept for fourteen hours straight.

When she woke, whole sections of her work plan were overdue. Tasks blinked red and demanded to be time-shifted. She could grab them all and shove them into tomorrow, but it would cause more problems down the line. She needed to prioritize, delegate, problem-solve, but she couldn't bear to think about project management. Not after what had happened.

Ten years back, she'd been a good project manager—hadn't she? She'd always thought so. Prided herself on it, in fact. But if she'd ever had the skills to run a large project, they'd atrophied from disuse.

Or maybe she'd always been a disaster. Yes. Six dead people proved it.

Minh sat on the beach, running analyses on the climate data until she was feeling normal again. She picked her microclimate survey points and assigned cameras and sensors to their positions. The sun was about to rise in Mesopotamia, and when it did, she'd supervise the vegetation surveys. Anything that couldn't be automatically identified or was likely to have significant genetic variation from samples in seed banks would be prioritized for sampling, and their locations would inform the choice of the next landing site.

But when the Mesopotamian dawn came and the cameras shifted from low-lux mode into full color, Minh stepped away from the feeds. Those sunlit vistas took her right back to the barley field, the soldiers splashing to the ground, the sickening scent of burning green barley and fertile mud. She stared at the ocean and let the surveys run unmonitored.

Hamid sat in the sand at her side. He handed her a bowl of food and a water bottle. They ate in silence. Minh could only swallow a few bites. The food sat under her heart in a lump.

Hamid's bowl was half empty before he finally spoke. "Listen, Minh. I don't like what you've been doing to your endocrine system."

"It's none of your business," she said. "Stay out of my biom."

"Okay. But I need you to be more careful. If you hadn't reduced your adrenaline, fear would have kicked in properly and brought you back to the skip without cutting it so close."

Minh nodded. Her eyes prickled. She pinched the bridge of her nose, like she'd been doing all day. The flood would have to break through eventually.

Hamid dug his toes into the sand.

"According to TERN, past population members don't die, not really," he said. "This is a new baseline. When we leave, the timeline will collapse. When TERN comes back, those soldiers will be alive."

Minh pulled her legs into a ball. "It's a comforting thought."

"You don't look comfortable."

"That's because I don't buy it. Do you?"

He gave a gentle laugh, and his eyes disappeared behind a web of wrinkles in his weathered face.

"Ah, Minh. You know me."

"Yeah," she said. "You only care about animals."

"I wouldn't put it that way, but as far as I'm concerned, human deaths are nothing compared to the mass extinctions. Bringing back animal populations is worth a few human lives. More than a few."

"Would you have been okay if I'd died?"

"No, I'd be devastated."

"What's the difference between the soldiers killing me, and Fabian killing the soldiers? Why would I be more dead than them?"

"If you died, we couldn't go back in time and find you alive again."

"Can't we? Can't TERN travel forty years into the past? Or two weeks? They could grab me out of the past and put me right back into the present."

Hamid looked thoughtful. "I suppose. But we would all know you'd died."

"Exactly. Like those soldiers died. They're not less dead because we don't know their names." Minh swirled her legs, stirring the sand under her. "I'm sure TERN has a tangle of metaphysics justifying their health and safety protocol. I bet their physicists split time travel hairs down to the nanometer, in that awful hell of theirs. But right here, right now, the plain fact is—"

We're on an island with a killer.

She bit the words back. Hamid would lock down her biom and dial her full of sedatives. And he'd be right to do it. She was overwrought.

And it wasn't Fabian's fault the soldiers were dead. It was her fault.

She dialed herself down, and calm closed over her like

a warm blanket. Her gut unclenched. She scrubbed her hands through her hair. She should have cut it before leaving Calgary. She watched Hamid through the shaggy locks hanging in her eyes. He looked tense, like he was expecting her to say something irredeemable.

"The plain fact is we're here to do a job," she said. "We'll finish what we came here to do, go home, file the final report, invoice the client, and move on to the next job."

Saying it made it true.

~

Minh immersed herself in her work. She time-shifted the work plan and then dived into the live remote feeds. The vegetation survey was engrossing, the cultivated areas of the landscape as biodiverse as the wild. Plants and landscape, rocks and lichen, water and algae, pure and simple.

Eight camera feeds filled her eye. When humans strayed into the survey areas, the cameras avoided them, either zipping to a new location or rising high overhead. The cameras were usually spotted—pointed at, exclaimed over, chased, but it didn't matter. Cameras couldn't hurt anyone.

In a vineyard survey, a woman in a pink tunic padded barefoot down a dusty track. When she spotted the camera, she raised her arm and part of her costume flew off.

Minh maximized the feed and scanned backward in slow motion. A dark winged mass flew back and latched onto the woman's arm. Minh zoomed in. A small falcon perched on the woman's leather wrist cuff. When Minh jumped back to the live camera feed, outstretched talons raked at the lens, reaching for Minh's eye. The camera dropped low and looped behind the bird, trapping a close-up of the bird's fanned tailfeathers quivering in the wind.

The falconer recalled the bird to her wrist with a sharp whistle. She stared up at Minh's camera, eyes narrow, jaw tight, lips drawn into a thin line.

The falconer snatched a stone from the track and pitched it. The camera dodged easily. Minh sent it up to two hundred meters and paused the survey. It could wait until the falconer moved on.

Minh bookmarked the incident and shot the feed to Hamid and Kiki. Hamid got back to her right away with more information about the bird's species than she wanted to know, but Kiki didn't reply. When Minh climbed up to the cubbies—late, too late, she'd worked too long into the night—Kiki's cubby was sealed. So was Hamid's. Fabian's was empty.

Kiki hadn't whispered to her all day. She'd been working hard—the work breakdown was thick with her timestamps. A day ago, Minh would have said Kiki couldn't go an hour without chattering at her.

Now, it appeared, Kiki had pulled away. The trust was gone. It left a hole, right under her ribs. Minh curled up in her cubby and wondered when she'd begun caring what Kiki thought of her.

-15-

A SILVER STONE CIRCLED overhead, moving lightly as a bubble in the breeze. Its red eye glinted, watching him. Shulgi tried to keep it in sight, but it settled directly overhead. If he kept looking up like a pheasant gaping at the clouds, he'd leave himself open to attack. He ignored it for now and returned his attention to the ditch where the monster waited for him.

The monster's egg was broken cleanly in half, the open sides cupping the earth. A material like sea-foam oozed from under the broken sides.

Demons, monsters, spirits, and ghouls had once been common, but that age had passed. In Shulgi's lifetime, they were only vague rumors and well-worn stories. Everyone claimed to know someone who'd seen them, but when his falconers tracked those rumors to the source, they lost all substance. Until now.

Shulgi's duty was to protect the land from all threats. In dreams, he'd battled monsters, sometimes losing, rarely winning, but often the dream-monsters disappeared or transformed before the battle resolved. Few of the battles felt real, though the priests claimed he was fighting in a spirit realm where force and motion were unpredictable.

Shulgi was dubious. Everyone dreamed. Most of the time it meant nothing.

Killing the octopus-woman might not be difficult. It was clumsy. Easily frightened, too. This might be Shulgi's only opportunity to exercise his duty. He'd be sure to kill it with proper ceremony.

~

Kiki changed. She did her work and kept the fab humming, but the cheerful, companionable chatter was gone. No jokes, no whispering, no teasing. Minh should have been too busy to notice, too focused on work to care, but she tracked Kiki's movements, as surely as if she were tagged with a monitoring camera.

Just good project management, she told herself. *Keeping an eye on the junior team member.*

Kiki was getting cozy with Fabian. He'd set up a hammock on the far side of the island, and Kiki wandered over there often, disappearing for hours at a time.

After lunch, Minh watched Kiki gather up the dishes and toss them to the hygiene bot, then trot under the palms to the beach.

"I didn't think we'd have to worry about our research assistant defecting to the other side," Minh said, nudging the whirring bot with her toe.

Hamid was abstracted, running multiple streams, attention only half in the present moment.

"It's a good move for her," he answered. "More options with TERN than in Calgary, if she can catch Fabian's eye."

A cold stone dropped into Minh's stomach. "You don't think they . . ."

"A romance?" He shrugged. "I don't know. I have no time for primate behavior right now. But it's clear there's something going on."

"Kiki's asexual."

"She cut off her legs to get this one chance at time travel. What do you think she'd do to make a career out of it?"

The next morning, when Fabian finally rolled out of his cubby, Minh followed him to the other side of the island. His hammock hung between two palm trees, overlooking a slender sickle of white beach bordering water that shaded from turquoise to cobalt a few meters from shore. The sand was pocked with Kiki's hoofprints, half washed away by the rain.

"I hope you're not tasking Kiki with any of your historian workflow," she said as Fabian shook the water out of his hammock.

"Not a chance. The three of you are the most boring time travelers in the world, so I have plenty of time for research."

He pried open his breakfast container and scooped a spoonful into his mouth.

"But I shouldn't complain," he added. "Can you imagine the drama a doc crew gets into? It's a pain in the ass, but it makes the time go by fast."

Minh drew herself up to her full height. "I didn't realize we were here to entertain you."

"Humans can't help but be entertaining." His lips parted in a faint sneer. "Most of them, anyway."

"Luckily, you've got a whole world full of people at your fingertips."

"Yes. Lucky me."

He sat on his hammock, legs dangling, and fired a live feed onto the horizon. The sour-faced priestess perched on the edge of a golden chair in a dim courtyard, eyes closed, hands folded in her lap. Lamplight flickered over her face. Her eyelids and lips quivered as she muttered to herself.

"What can I do for you, Minh?" asked Fabian.

Minh pointed at the feed. "I suppose this is what you've been sharing with Kiki."

"She lurks when she has time. I bookmark the interesting bits for her."

The audio feed picked up the quick whisper of the woman's breath, the tinkle of water in the fountain at her feet. Minh zoomed in on her face. Lamplight glinted on the golden jewelry around the woman's collarbones.

"Who is she?"

"Susa, priestess of the moon. She's praying. Lots to worry about right now in her world. Monsters in a barley field. Disks floating around the landscape. New stars appearing in the night sky."

Six dead soldiers, Minh thought.

"I suppose there's no way to explain," she said softly.

"No point." He pulled his legs into the hammock. "We'll be gone soon."

"Listen, I want to find the safest possible location for the next landing."

"It won't be a problem. Choose whatever location you want. Nobody will bother us."

Minh took a sharp breath. The conversation had been going so well. Now Fabian was talking nonsense.

"Come on, Minh." He laughed. "What do you think I've been doing out here, working on my tan? I've been brushing up on my Akkadian. Lots of lexical shifts in the past two hundred years, but she's been helping me." He gestured at the priestess.

Minh stared at him. "You're kidding."

"When we time travel, we don't sit around and record

stuff. We gather data and analyze it, same as you. I'm making friends with her. She'll help make our next landing much easier."

"You'll tell her to make sure everyone stays away from us?"

"I'll hand down the law. Don't look so worried."

"Then why didn't you do that on the first landing?" She could throttle him. Grab his skinny neck and squeeze until his teeth popped out.

"We needed to get the cameras and bugs into place. And I'm still working on the language."

Her vision dimmed as her blood pressure dropped. She dialed herself up and her pressor response surged. Her face turned hot with rage. If she flipped the hammock, he'd be on the ground and helpless.

"Want to meet her?" Fabian didn't wait for an answer. He adjusted the feed so the priestess appeared to be sitting in front of them. "Say hi, Susa."

The priestess stood. She raised her left arm and opened her hand, waving awkwardly. Her eyes scanned the rooftops, searching for a point to fix on.

"Shu-lu-mu," the priestess said in a gravelly voice.

"You're not talking to her," Minh said. "Not directly."

"No, I'm using a morphological parser and a syntax database. But I didn't have to start from square one. We have a pretty good handle on Akkadian."

"You told her to stand up and wave. And she did it because she thinks you're—what? A god?"

Fabian looked a little shamefaced. "Yes."

Minh nodded. "Okay. Okay, you're a god. I guess we're all gods, compared to these people. Where's the bug?"

Susa raised her hand to her hair and withdrew a tiny black sphere pinched between her thumb and forefinger. She held it out for a moment before replacing it.

"She can make her people do whatever you want?" Minh asked.

"Susa's powerful," he said. "Second only to the king."

"She'll tell them to keep away from us. Good. What else? Can you make them bring us arthropod samples?"

"I guess so, sure. Can you be more specific?"

"Ask her for worms. Insects. Spiders. Snails and slugs. Eggs and larvae, too—especially aquatic specimens. Mollusks—everything they can find. We want a few of each individual type, not thousands of one kind. Can you do that?"

Fabian grinned. "Now you're starting to think like a time traveler."

-16-

A THUMPING SOUNDED FROM inside the egg. The monster spoke: *Shit-shit-shit-shit-shit-shit-where-are-your-health-and-safety-protocols-now.*

Shulgi strained to understand the words.

I'm-the-child-of-your-child's-child's-child.

It laughed. A human sound, but demented. Perhaps it would attack now. He readied his weapons.

～

Minh added a manual arthropod biodiversity survey to the workflow—no analysis, only collection and cataloguing. The samples would have no provenance, no metadata, but it wouldn't be the first time she'd had to work with incomplete information. It was better than nothing. Arthropods had been an unsolvable problem, but now they were a research management hassle.

She filled Kiki's work breakdown with fab tasks. They needed hundreds of sample jars, in all sizes, stackable, airtight, sterile. And it would keep Kiki away from Fabian.

Minh paced around the fab. "We need cellular fixative to preserve the samples. Formalin isn't much more than formaldehyde in solution. Easy."

Kiki looked up from the humming fab. "This kind of fab can't print liquids."

"But you can make the equipment to make liquids."

"Technically, yes. Let me see." The skin under Kiki's left eye twitched. "To make formaldehyde, we need alcohol. I could make a still. Where do you want to get the carbohydrates?"

Minh looked around. "Palm trees?"

"Do you really want me to fab a chain saw and start cutting down trees?"

"No, that's ridiculous. Can't you print carbohydrates?"

"Not while I'm making sample jars."

"Why didn't we bring any alcohol with us?"

Kiki shrugged and turned back to monitor the fab as it chugged out sample jars.

Minh scrubbed her fingers through her hair. This was getting out of hand.

"Most samples can be stored dry," Minh said to Kiki's back. "Soft-bodied specimens can go into a saline solution."

"Salt water." Kiki didn't turn around.

"Not perfect, but we're improvising."

"A lot of improvising going on," Kiki said under her breath.

Kiki stacked a row of tiny jars onto the rack she'd fabbed earlier. Two dozen jars took nearly twenty minutes to create. They didn't even have lids.

"How do you want to sterilize these?" Kiki asked. Her back was still turned.

"You'll have to fab a dry-heat sterilizer. Easy. Why is this taking so long?"

Kiki plopped a jar into Minh's hand. "This fab isn't optimized for small, fine work. It chokes on the jar threads."

"Then make a different kind of container."

Kiki rounded on her, eyes narrowed. "You said make jars."

"Make whatever fabs fastest. It doesn't matter, as long as it's airtight."

By the time they were ready for the second landing, Kiki had filled every corner of the skip with jars, tubs, cartons, and containers. When Minh strapped into her seat, Kiki dumped a bandolier of test tubes in her lap. They were still hot from the sterilizer.

Two minutes into the upskip, Hamid was snoring as usual. Behind him, Kiki was asleep, too, long arms softly drifting. Fabian was head-down in the feeds, unfocused eyes hidden behind mirrored sunglasses. He'd promised to keep close tabs on their landing site, and Minh dropped into his feed whenever she could, to make sure health and safety was top priority in his workflow. Their second landing was scheduled to last thirty-six hours, and Minh didn't want lose one moment on the ground.

She glanced at her workflows. Her analyses were running well, with climate data funneling in from the micro-climate sites, and biodiversity survey cameras running their programs efficiently. The microscopic floating gauges she'd released into the Euphrates were beginning to illuminate the rivers with hydrometric and water temperature data. The gauges were flowing into the Tigris through the narrow canals joining the two rivers, and were making their way up into the tributaries, through the canals, the ponds, irrigation ditches, and reservoirs, and down to the coastal wetlands. The data was still patchy, but the numbers looked solid.

The instream biodiversity survey was another matter. High levels of suspended sediment kept the underwater cameras from trapping visual data, so the seers extrapolated species from infrared and sonar. A lot of gaps in those data sets.

Minh checked her queue. It was packed with bookmarks, mostly from Hamid. She flipped through them and got an eyeful of horse docs, full data trapped from multiple angles. A dizzying parade of animals grazing, laboring under harness and saddle, or lazing in the shade.

She dove into the biota survey feeds. More horses.

She flicked a sharp toe across Hamid's shoulder.

Have you looked at anything other than horses since we got here?

Hamid snorted, then nestled back against his headrest, hand over his eyes. His fake hove into view. It smirked.

I knew you were going to say that. Take a closer look.

It tossed her a metadata catalog. Hamid's portion of the biota survey was ahead of target, with hundreds of species recorded and prioritized for the sampling wasps. But when she rifled through the bookmarks, all she saw were horses. She shook her head and looked closer. No, the catalogued species were there with the horses. A fox slipping behind the hocks of a dozing mare to nab a field mouse. A crested lark hopping across a pair of brown haunches. A tall heron fishing in the shallows with a mare and foal in the pasture beyond. Sheep in a dawn-lit corral, nosing a few flakes of grain from the dirt beside a horse hoof.

Hamid had found a way to do his work and feed his horse obsession at the same time.

You're sneaky.

Thanks, boss. The fake tipped its ridiculous hat and faded away.

Fabian had sent her bookmarks, too. Violent ones, showing the faces of brutality—cold, heartless, bloody.

Screaming fights witnessed through windows. Men beating men, men beating women, both beating children, all of them beating animals.

Fabian's message was clear. No point in sympathizing with past population members. They get what they deserve.

It was enough for Minh. She flushed the whole stack.

Only three bookmarks from Kiki. One showed a crowded open-air pottery workshop, the artisans chattering to each other as they sweated in the heat from a glowing kiln. Another showed a row of children in the shade of a plane tree, poking sticks into wads of clay under the watchful eye of a stooped oldster. The third bookmark showed a pair of people lazing in a blanket-strewn alcove, holding hands and chatting quietly. If Hamid's passion was horses, and Fabian was fixated on violence, Minh supposed what Kiki really cared about was people.

A harmless obsession, she figured.

Minh reached back into her history and pulled up the falconer bookmark. The pink tunic's color signature was distinctive; she grabbed the string and ran a search through the past few days of data.

Easy. Yesterday, a camera had trapped the falconer in the background of the vegetation survey, perched on a wall, eating bread smeared with something greasy. It dripped down her chin and blotched her tunic, then the camera moved on.

Minh cross-referenced the time and location on the previous day's satellite feed and ran the feed backward, tracking the falconer to a mud brick shack in a village surrounded by vineyards and orchards. Then she grabbed that morning's satellite feed and tagged the falconer as she left the house. The feed zipped ahead, tracing her route through the fields. The falconer's long shadow shortened as the sun rose. The bird flew from her wrist and snapped back like a toy on a rubber band.

The satellite feed shuddered into real time. The falconer was striding through a riverside village. Minh grabbed the nearest camera and sent it spinning toward her.

By the time the camera arrived, a gang of farmers surrounded the falconer. They were clearly upset, throwing their arms around and yelling, but the falconer didn't seem worried. She listened patiently, scuffing her foot in the red dirt and waggling her head from side to side in a gesture that appeared to be the local version of a nod.

A child spotted Minh's camera and yelped. Heads turned, jaws dropped, but before the crowd could erupt into chaos, the falconer barked an order. The farmers formed a ragged line and clasped their hands in front of their bare bellies.

The falconer turned and stared into Minh's eyes. She

was about the same age as Kiki, and like Kiki, her skin glowed with that impossible sheen of youth, marred by a few tiny imperfections: a pale scar on her chin, and a constellation of shallow pockmarks on her cheeks.

She'd been through a plague of her own, this one.

Minh turned the camera toward the farmers. Thumb-to-thumb and finger-to-finger, their navels peeked out from between their hands like pupils in a line of shadowed eyes.

We see you, the gesture clearly said. *Go away.*

I see you, too. Minh tipped the camera from side to side, mimicking the waggling nod the falconer had made moments earlier. Then she let the camera go back to its survey.

THE SILVER STONE WHIPPED past Shulgi's face. He barely restrained himself from flailing at it with his weapons. In the ditch, mud sloshed.

No-no-no-no-no-no-hamid-wake-up-wake-up-shit-shit-shit.

The monster was gone, but snakelike trails showed it had run across the ditch and squeezed itself into the other half of the egg. It had used the silver stone to distract him, like a dog harrying a lion to let a hunter close in. Clever.

~

Hamid woke as they dropped into the downskip. He leaned toward Minh across the skip's narrow aisle. "You finally looked at my bookmarks," he said.

Minh pinned him with a narrow squint. "You made equids your focal taxon."

His eyes went wide; feigned innocence beamed across the cramped skip cabin.

"No, but horses do seem to be a keystone species in this ecosystem."

"How surprising."

"That means the client's project won't be complete unless horses are strongly represented among the restored species."

"Even if they start the restoration tomorrow, you'd be long gone before it gets to that point."

"I don't need to see it, as long as it happens." He grinned.

Behind Minh, Fabian was deep in his feeds. She tapped a toe on his knee.

"Are you joining us for this landing?"

Fabian reached under his sunglasses and scrubbed his knuckles over his eyes.

"The site looks good," he said. "No surprises."

Minh shot him the feed showing the farmers holding their thumbs and fingers in front of their bellies.

"What does this gesture mean?"

"Superstition. A ward against demons. It's related to the evil eye."

"They think we're evil?"

"Aren't we?" mumbled Kiki. She was still slumped in her seat, eyes closed.

"No," Fabian said flatly. "We're here to do a job and leave."

"We know that, but they don't." Kiki stretched. Her hooves bumped the back of Hamid's seat.

"Debate this with your time travel ethics tutor," Fabian said. "Let me know how long it stays interesting. I'm betting ten minutes max."

Minh's toes curled into fists. She wrenched herself around in her seat.

"Fabian, are you poaching our research assistant?"

"They grow up so fast," Hamid said under his breath.

Fabian was unconcerned. "Yell at me later. I'm running health and safety now."

Minh turned to Kiki. *Are you leaving Calgary?*

Kiki glared at her. "Oh, are you talking to me again?"

Minh strengthened her grip on the string of test tubes, steadying it against the increasing pressure of their descent.

"Why wouldn't I talk to you?"

"Your fake has been treating me like dirt ever since the first landing."

Minh checked her dash. Her fake had been running its default workflow, intercepting and rejecting every attempt at private communication from Kiki.

"I forgot to turn off my fake. An oversight."

"No, it's business as usual. I'm just the admin who nags you to approve invoices and review RFPs before the business meeting. I'm no better than a fake, and that'll never change, no matter how hard I work or how well I do my job. Will it?"

"Can we talk about this later? We're landing in a minute."

"Will it?" Kiki pounded her fist on the armrest.

"Now, kids," Hamid said softly.

Fabian watched them intently, gaze flickering from Kiki to Minh and back again.

Are you enjoying this? she whispered to him. *A little drama to make the days go faster?*

Minh turned back to Kiki. "I can't change hab economics. I wish ESSA could give you more work, but we barely stay afloat."

"You don't get it, do you? You have no idea why the fat babies are leaving the habs."

"Things are hard. You're giving up."

"We're giving up? Us?" Kiki leaned across the aisle, straining against her safety restraints as the skip settled into landing position. "No, the plague babies have given up. You used to believe in something, but now all you want to do is service the banks."

Fabian cracked the hatch. "Cameras up."

"We'd work for free," Kiki said. "Every last one of us, to learn what you know."

"You can't do that. Calgary's economy would plummet."

"You sound like a banker, Minh."

"I'm not—"

"The economy is an excuse. The truth is, you built the habs for yourselves and created us as pets. We were cute when we were little, but now you don't know what to do with us. You feed us on scraps."

"Boots down," Fabian said.

Kiki shucked her restraints. She paused in the hatchway, backlit by the morning sun.

"You've given up on the future. So, when we leave, don't blame us. Blame yourself."

-18-

SHULGI GLIMPSED MOVEMENT IN a distant stand of lemon trees. His soldiers—yes—one of them waved. He would wait another minute or two and then confront the monster.

The octopus woman might be cowardly, but she was powerful, too. She had many clever allies. Silver stones had been spotted all over the kingdom—hundreds of them. At Asnear, she'd been protected by a burr-like creature that slayed soldiers on a whim, and she'd been accompanied by three other monsters he hadn't yet spotted. Perhaps they were hiding, too.

And even if the octopus woman was alone—weren't those legs useful? Was it born a chimera, or created from a person? If born, perhaps the children could be raised as proper humans. If created, Shulgi might pursue the transformation himself. What couldn't he do with four extra limbs!

~

The second landing site was a narrow spit extending into the wide lower Tigris. This part of the river was a geological newborn, formed from sediment laid down when the Tigris split from its confluence with the Euphrates only a few centuries earlier. But Minh hadn't chosen it for its geology. She'd picked it because the flat terrain gave long sight lines broken only by a few tamarisk and mulberry trees.

Minh took her samples automatically, paying no attention to the quality of the mud, the suck and pull of the sampling mechanism, the layers of sediment revealed within the cores, or the wiggling benthic organisms dredged up by the dragnets. For more than half a century, she'd focused her life on rocks, mud, dirt, and the things that lived and grew in and around flowing water. She'd never seen such richness, the riverbanks festooned with flowering forbs and buzzing with pollinating insects, the cool, sediment-laden water flowing through deep pools, the gravel shallows rippling with fry. She should have been fascinated by the landscape, eager to see if her core samples penetrated to the old substrate, but she couldn't concentrate.

All she wanted to do was go back up to the skip and yell at Kiki until she promised not to leave Calgary.

You can dump your armor, Fabian whispered. *Aren't you hot?*

Irritation washed over Minh. *I'm fine.*

Then why are you looking over your shoulder every twenty seconds?

If you've got free time, why don't you assist Hamid with the biodiversity inventory?

I'm helping Kiki pack up the bugs.

Of course he was. Fabian would take every opportunity to get his hooks in deeper.

By the time Minh finished her sampling, her shadow had shrunk to a flat disk underfoot. A pair of lizards stretched on a flat rock at the edge of the riverbank, dozing in the heat. Her biom blinked a hydration warning. She should go back to the skip, eat, rehydrate. But she'd worked straight through the morning. Time to stop and enjoy the river.

Minh sent her floats back to the skip and waded into the channel, the thick sediment squelching underfoot. She floated over the thalweg, took a deep breath, and let the water close over her head like a helmet. Birdsong was replaced by the deep, persistent pulse of river flow.

No point in opening her eyes, not with all that sediment, but she could still see. She pulled data from all the local floaters, assigned glowing avatars to the datapoints, and threw it into a spatial mock-up.

The simulation had her surrounded. Three mature silver carp ranged upstream, followed by a small Ganges shark. Nine unidentified organisms browsed the riverbed, probably juvenile catfish. Nearly a hundred smolts sheltered under the bankside root system at the far edge of a deep pool. A softshell turtle dug in the mud with its front flippers, hunting worms and nymphs. All this within a five-meter radius. The river glimmered with life.

Minh swam up and down the reach, working on her riparian ecosystem classification and ignoring her biom until it slid a flashing nutritional demand into the middle of her eye. As she ran back to the skip, a raptor circled overhead. It was probably watching Hamid, waiting to swoop down and pick off one of his fleeing rodents.

Minh grabbed a lunch pack out of the skip and headed toward the tent.

Fabian's pet priestess had erected a tiered pedestal of mud bricks that raised the tent's floor a half meter off the ground. From each of the four corners, copper-banded, curved wooden struts braced wool walls shot through with gold and festooned with shiny metal discs, bright tassels of yarn, and painted clay flowers.

Inside, rugs lay on patterned tiles. Dappled light cast patterns over Kiki and Fabian, who sat on low stools among inlaid tables piled high with boxes and bowls, reed cages and covered pots, baskets and vases, and tippy little metal tripods hanging with cloth and leather bags.

"How are the samples?" Minh asked.

Kiki jumped. She fumbled a sample jar. It rolled under a table.

"We were just saying you need an entomologist to do this properly," said Fabian.

"A herpetologist, too." Kiki pointed at a dozen covered baskets stacked at the far end of the tent. "Those are snakes. I'm not going anywhere near them. Fabian says they're venomous."

"Nice," said Minh. "Did we ask for snakes?"

Fabian palmed a box off one of the tables and cracked its lid.

"We asked for everything," he said.

"Is Susa trying to kill us?"

Fabian tipped the box's contents into a test tube. A beetle slid out, legs scrambling.

"She probably thought we could handle a few snakes," he said. "She thinks we're gods, remember?"

Kiki popped snails into a jar of saline.

"You could tell Susa the truth," she said. "Explain why we're here. People are smart. They can handle it."

Fabian began to answer, but then his gaze flickered up to Minh and his mouth snapped shut.

"Don't mind me." Minh faked a smile.

Fabian looked wary. Minh glided over to the nearest table and scanned the jugs and bins. A wide-mouthed jar

Kelly Robson

was sealed with a layer of clay. She broke it with the tip of her toe. Ants swarmed out, carrying white pupae in their jaws. Her seer sputtered, unable to identify the species.

Minh scooped up a sample jar. If she kept quiet, maybe Fabian would say something stupid.

"You can't explain time travel to preindustrial past population members," he said. "They have no sense of history and no vocabulary for talking about time outside the lifespan of a few generations."

"They understand ancestors and descendants," said Kiki. "I would say, 'I'm your child's child's child many times over.' They'd get it."

"Assuming they don't kill you while you're waiting for the translation matrix to find the right syntax?"

"Assuming I haven't frightened them, yes."

"In every past population, children are expected to honor and obey their parents. Even adult children. What are you going to do when three or four generations start bossing you around while you're trying to check boxes on your work breakdown? How will you get your project done?"

"Easy. I'd get them to help me."

Fabian snorted. "You have no idea what families are like."

Or what project management is like, Minh thought as she tried to scoop ants into a sample jar. They were crawling all over her. The vinegary sting of formic acid prickled her nostrils.

"We don't come here to get adopted into an extended family," Fabian continued. "We come here to work, so keep it simple. Use whatever strategy lets you get your project done."

Those words could have come out of Minh's own mouth. Fabian was putting on a show for her. She had to get out of the tent.

Minh capped the sample jar and brushed the ants out of her hair.

"Do you want me to take care of these snakes?" she asked.

"Yes, please." Kiki shuddered. "Can you take them away—far away?"

"Sure. Across the river if you want."

I'd like to keep listening in, though, Minh whispered. She shot Kiki a request to lurk on her feed.

The snake baskets were awkward. Minh piled them on the float as best she could, and then climbed aboard, holding them secure with all her legs as the float staggered under the weight. The snakes shifted beneath her, alarmed by the movement, throwing their heavy bodies against the sides of their baskets.

When Kiki accepted Minh's lurk request, her visuals were focused on a leather bucket of earthworms. Minh threw the feed into the upper right corner of her eye.

"You think I'm naïve." Kiki's tone was low, confidential.

"You're an amateur," said Fabian. "TERN's ethics specialists think about nothing else all day long. And you know what? They're miserable. Time travel ethics is a dead-end field."

"Doing the right thing is important."

"No, doing the right thing is impossible."

Kiki groaned. "You're so cynical."

"No, I'm not. A cynical person can think up a hundred good reasons not to get out of bed in the morning. But there's one good reason to time travel, and it overrules every objection." Fabian sounded like himself again—overbearing, know-it-all, priggish.

Minh guided the float over the river and set it down gently on the wide, sandy bank. When the snakes settled down, she tiptoed into the water, stretched out one leg, and tipped the first basket. A slender snake slipped out. Minh's seer identified it as a horned viper, but Hamid already had a sample from the species, so she let it slither into the rocks unmolested.

"Can you guess what the reason is?" Fabian asked. Kiki didn't answer. "Do you want a hint?"

"I'm thinking," Kiki said.

The next snake's glossy black body was thick as Minh's

wrist. She tagged it and a sample wasp chased it up the bank.

"You time travel because you can, like the plague babies who climb mountains. Because it's there," Kiki said. "Fine. I'm not saying don't do it. But there's got to be a better way than dropping skips on people's heads."

The next snake struck at Minh's leg. She tossed it into a patch of purple irises. A sample wasp buzzed its cloaca.

"Using skips to transfer project teams from safe bases to hot spots is the best strategy we've found," Fabian said. "If you find a better approach, let me know. I won't hold my breath."

Minh could almost smell the smugness oozing off him.

"If you could see the long-term consequences of your actions, you wouldn't be so casual about it." Kiki slipped a palm-sized moth into a petri dish.

"TERN's actions have no consequences for past population members. But their actions have consequences for us."

"I'm not sure the timeline-collapse theory isn't a convenient excuse for doing whatever you want."

Fabian laughed. "If I could do anything I wanted, I wouldn't be sorting through a bag of maggots right now."

"I'm serious."

"Unless you want to go to the other side of the curve and spend the next twenty years as a physics apprentice, you'll have to take my word for it."

"I might do that, if I got the chance," Kiki said. "It sounds like important work."

Minh fumed. How could Kiki stand it? How could any of the fat babies stand it? Going back underground, living together like ants, everyone in each other's business, never seeing another horizon, another sunrise or sunset?

Minh tipped over the last three baskets. The snakes coiled into striking positions. She splashed through the river and ran back to camp.

She'd shake sense into Kiki, even if she had to wring her neck to do it.

Minh lunged up the tent platform steps, breathing heavily, ready to start bellowing. But Kiki was waiting, her face dark and pitiless as a thunderhead.

Kiki handed Minh a sample jar. A huge grasshopper was propped diagonally inside the cylinder, scraping its stridulatory file and beating its wings.

"I want to do important work," Kiki said, and the light that shone from those clear, bright eyes was too intense. Minh looked away.

"That's all any of us want. To not go to waste," Kiki said.

-19-

***KIKI-NO*, THE MONSTER SOBBED**. *Where-are-you.*

It sounded like a real person as it cried.

The soldiers were close. Shulgi slid into the ditch, crouched in front of the egg, and peered inside. It was half-filled with sea-foam. From one of the walls protruded a white cocoon-like chair. A small man dangled from it, unconscious, his hips and legs embedded in pebbly white material. Or at least, he looked like a man. He might well be a monster. In any case, he was diseased—a massive tumor bulged under his jaw.

~

Minh swam downstream, trailed by a train of floats. The setting sun turned the brown river into a molten stream of gold. She'd spent the afternoon taking benthic samples. Hours alone, unobserved, except for the raptor circling overhead.

At least the bird couldn't listen in on her thoughts.

The cool water soothed her aching shoulders and

back. She was already getting stiff, her range of movement restricted, so she reached into her biom and dialed up a general anti-inflammatory. A hit of serotonin-norepinephrine would take care of the ache deep below her breastbone, too, but she'd never relied on the happy hormones, and she wasn't going to start now.

Besides, she deserved that pain. She'd failed. They'd all failed—all the plague babies, her entire generation. They'd tried to make a better world, but forgotten who they were making it for.

No wonder Kiki couldn't forgive her.

After stowing her samples in the *Peach,* she joined her team at the campfire and opened her supper container. Kiki and Fabian sat on cushions they'd dragged from the tent. Evening stars glinted overhead.

Hamid appeared in the distance, a dark shape looming beside him. Four legs. It tossed its head.

Minh jumped up. "Shit."

"Did you see Hamid got himself a pet?" Fabian asked.

"The horse didn't get here by itself," she snapped.

"A kid brought it," said Fabian. "They've run off now, back home."

Minh pulled up Hamid's feed. He crouched at the horse's chest, reins in one hand, running his other hand over its slender foreleg.

Hamid, this wasn't in the work breakdown.

He kicked her off his feed. The window blinked out.

"Shit," she said.

Kiki and Fabian exchanged a look. They'd probably been whispering about her all day.

"Have fun camping," she said. "I'll sleep in the *Peach*. Tell Hamid not to fall in love with the horse, because we can't take it home."

She reclined her seat, took another hit of anti-inflammatory, and dialed herself asleep.

A few hours before dawn, the local floaters alerted her to a new species. No visuals, not in the murky water and certainly not at night. But they were large—sturgeon, maybe. She batted groggily at the feeds, trying to make sense of them. No, they were mammals, six of them, moving slowly upriver. Finless porpoise, maybe, or river dolphin. She'd look closer in the morning.

Minh's alarm woke her at first light. She was itchy, her skin gritty. No matter. She'd be back in the river soon enough. Maybe they should all get in the river before they left, or it would be a stinky trip back to Home Beach. Hamid would smell like horse. As usual.

She stretched and checked her feeds. The mammals were still there, six datapoints resting near the surface of the upstream pool. She sent a camera but nothing was visible from the surface, not even in low-lux mode.

Fabian and Kiki were awake. Minh scooped four

breakfast packs out of the heat exchange brought them to the fireside. Hamid trotted into camp on horseback. He leaned down, plucked his breakfast out of Minh's hand, and cantered off.

"I guess everyone's up," Minh said.

"Susa's up, too. She's on her way," said Fabian.

"What?" said Minh. She wasn't sure she'd heard.

"Susa is coming to visit." He fired a feed onto the horizon.

A narrow barge floated down the dark river. Golden lantern light shimmered on the water, brighter than the dim rays of dawn stretching overhead. The priestess stood in the boat's prow, gripping the rail, steadying herself as her head swayed from side to side under the weight of her wig. Servants and soldiers clustered behind her.

Ice slid down Minh's spine.

"No. That's not in the work plan," she said.

"It's in mine," said Fabian. "I gave up a whole day to wrangle insects. Now I've got my own work to do."

Minh turned to Kiki. "Did you know about this?"

Kiki nodded.

"Why didn't you tell me?" Minh's voice rose to a screech.

"There's no reason to worry," Fabian said around a mouthful of breakfast.

"They've got weapons. All of them—even the children."

"Susa will come alone."

"Their precious priest? Not a chance."

"If it gets out of hand, I'll take care of it."

"No, you won't." Kiki's voice was soft.

Fabian sighed. "No more fighting over health and safety, Kiki. I'm done."

"I'm done, too. I'm not letting you kill anyone."

He glazed over for a moment, then snapped back. His eyes narrowed with menace.

"Where are my drones?"

"Back at Home Beach. I unloaded them before the up-skip," Kiki said. "You've been too busy to notice, running multiple streams, chatting with Susa."

The breakfast container fell from his hand. Beige nutritional mix oozed over his shoe.

Minh's flesh prickled. Twenty hours they'd been on the ground, unprotected. They could be dead. Dead. Acid burned the back of her throat. She swallowed. No time to think; time to move.

"We're leaving." She kept her voice flat. "Let's get the samples loaded. How long until Susa's barge lands?" Fabian didn't answer. She prodded him in the ribs with a toe. "Set a contact timer."

Fabian shook his head as if trying to shake off cobwebs.

"Forty minutes. Thirty to be safe." He shot a count-down onto the horizon, then kicked the food off his foot and rounded on Kiki. "We're going to talk about this on the way home."

Kiki bared her teeth. "I thought you were done talking about health and safety."

Minh wrapped a leg around Kiki's arm and pulled her toward the tent.

"Argue later," she said. "We've got work to do."

Kiki wrenched her arm free. "That's your default re-action to everything, isn't it, Minh? Do the work. After Fabian killed those soldiers, you were nearly catatonic. And you never woke up, did you? You kept running your program. Like a bot."

Hamid, we have to leave, Minh whispered. *Say goodbye to the horse.*

Minh ran into the tent and loaded sample trays onto the floats. Fast. She could move fast. Two floats held them all. Outside the tent, Fabian and Kiki were toe-to-toe. She was taller than him, triple-jointed legs fully extended for the advantage of height. He balanced on the balls of his feet, knees slightly bent, shoulders low, hands loose. A fighter's stance.

"If you think you're joining TERN after this, you're wrong." His voice was deadly calm.

"I should walk away," Kiki said. "But no, I'll join TERN

and work toward changing your health and safety protocol."

He laughed. "We won't take you. Not after this."

"Oh, you'll take me." Kiki smiled down at him. "If you don't, I'll tell the world TERN kills people and pretends it doesn't matter."

"You signed a nondisclosure agreement."

"A huge fine. More debt. Who cares?"

"The Bank of Calgary would care. Multiple zeroes in the debit column. You understand what that means, right?"

Kiki didn't answer.

"Minh knows what it means," Fabian said. "Don't you, Minh?"

"No time to waste," Minh said as she stumbled down the tent platform. "We have to pack up. Kiki, can you go get Hamid?"

"Tell Kiki what would happen to Calgary if she broke her NDA."

"We'd never dig out from under that much debt," Minh said. "It would kill us."

"Nobody would die. It would just ruin Calgary's economy," Kiki said. "There's a difference."

"Enough," said Minh. "Go get Hamid off that horse."

Kiki didn't move. "Maybe going broke would be good for the plague babies. It'd force you to stop playing the

banking game and make hard decisions about the future."
She turned back to Fabian. "I'm not scared of your NDA,
so TERN can choose. Deal fairly with me, or everyone in
the world will know what you are."

Fabian balled his fists. Before he could lash out, Minh
grabbed Kiki around the waist and pulled her backward.
Kiki's hooves drummed the dirt.

Don't be stupid. If you think he's a killer—

He is!

*—why are you antagonizing him? Do you think he
wouldn't hesitate to kill you, too?*

Kiki's stopped struggling.

"Go get Hamid."

Kiki nodded and galloped off at full speed.

Fabian's expression was murderous, brow contracted,
jaw muscles bulging. Minh needed to talk him down. Say
something. Anything.

"Kiki's been playing with her hormonal mix," Minh
lied, voice silky. "If she doesn't calm down, Hamid will
lock her biom."

"You can keep your research assistant," he said, and
stalked into the tent.

Minh raised her hands to her throat. Her pulse hammered through her jugular, a few thin layers of muscle
and connective tissue below her skin. She dialed herself
down. Way down.

Time. They still had time. She clung to the side of the *Peach,* using four legs to stow the samples while keeping the countdown at the top of her visual field. When she was done, sixteen minutes were left on the clock. Hamid and Kiki were walking slowly toward camp, talking. He was still on horseback—of course he would keep the animal around for as long as possible.

Fabian was still in the tent. He probably needed more time to cool down. The skip was too small for fighting.

Sixteen minutes was enough time for a final look at the river. It might be her last chance. If Fabian grounded them for the rest of the project, she wouldn't blame him.

The sun was a thin neon fingernail reaching over the indigo hills. A deer splayed its spindly legs and stooped to drink from the river. The pool's surface was smooth, but the six mammals were on the move, their datapoints heading toward the shallows. The physiology data was showing odd numbers. Probably a glitch caused by the sediment load.

Minh dropped to her belly ten meters from the river. Aquatic mammals had excellent eyesight, and she didn't want to risk scaring them off. She held her breath. There. A round head and broad back appeared, rippling the dark water as it wriggled toward the bank.

It crawled out of the river.

Minh could barely make sense of what she was seeing.

Long limbs. Supple skin, lighter in the middle of the body, darker at the ends. An unknown species, but how could that be? The size of a human.

It was human.

20

THE OCTOPUS-WOMAN LUNGED TOWARD him, reaching with two legs. Shulgi stepped back into a defensive posture, but it didn't attack. Its body slammed against the inside of the egg, its flesh meeting the wall with a muffled thunk. An object whooshed behind Shulgi's head. He lunged sideways.

Silver stones circled his head—five, now six. They moved in unison, whirling, dipping like dancers, as if they were puppets dangling from threads in the hands of an invisible performer. The monster's allies were trying to distract him.

He ignored them and tried to lift the egg. It wasn't heavy, just awkward. He'd need the help of his soldiers to flip it.

~

Minh scrambled backward as two more people climbed up the bank. Her legs tangled and she fell, hard. Then she got control of her legs and ran. Proximity alarms blasted. Fabian emerged from the tent and raced toward the *Peach*. Kiki and Hamid were already inside, waiting in the open hatch.

"Get in, what are you waiting for?" Minh screamed at Fabian.

Kiki hauled him up by the elbows. Minh launched herself at the hatch and dragged herself inside.

"Go go go go go go go," she yelled.

Hamid slammed the hatch. Fabian hit the launch workflow. Kiki fired the feeds onto the bulkhead.

The overhead satellite showed six people running toward them. They were naked and dripping wet, but with weapons in their hands, they were soldiers now. Two carried pairs of heavy-hafted lances with huge blades the shape of olive leaves. Two had bows and heavy bundles of arrows with bulky projectile tips. One brandished a net weighted with spikes.

The sixth—the one with the round head and broad back who'd crawled out of the mud like a primordial creature—he carried two weapons. A gleaming sword, the vicious blade kinked and curved like a scythe, and a flail, a drooping leather bouquet with flowers made of metal thorns.

Minh crouched over her seat, clutching the headrest and staring at the feeds. She'd seen no metal in the river. The sonar would have picked it up.

"Where did they get those weapons?" she said.

"Buried," said Fabian.

He copied the satellite feed, ran it back, and zoomed in. The tilt shift distorted the perspective: Minh in the background warped out of true, stumbling and falling, splayed on the ground. She struggled to stand, then fell again in a tangle of legs as five men dug in the sand at the edge of the bank. The sixth stood over them, shoulders square, bald head high, watching down his long nose as she turned and ran.

"That's Shulgi," said Kiki. "I recognize his face."

One of Shulgi's men put the sword in his hand, the flail in the other, like a medical tech handing instruments to a surgeon. Shulgi leapt up the bank and sprinted after her.

Minh's stomach flipped and she killed the feed. Didn't want to see how close he'd gotten to catching her. But she was safe in the *Peach* now, safe from six naked soldiers with Bronze Age weapons. Safe. And leaving.

Shulgi barked an order. A soldier swung his net overhead twice and released it. The weight of the spikes stretched the web tight as it flew through the air. It clattered on the fuselage. On the feed, the noise of forged bronze hitting the skip sounded like chattering birds, but the noise didn't penetrate inside the *Peach*.

"Where's the upskip, already?" Minh said. "Can we leave?"

"Minh," said Hamid calmly, "you have to fasten your harness."

She was still kneeling backward on her seat. She pulled herself around and clipped her harness, spine rigid with stress.

The two archers stood shoulder to shoulder, bows pointed down, hands loose. When the *Peach* lifted off, they raised their weapons in unison and let fly two thick-headed arrows. A dull thud resounded through the cabin.

"Lucky shot," said Fabian. "But we're out of range now."

"Did they even hit us?" Kiki asked. "At most they glanced off."

Fabian didn't answer. The upskip accelerated, momentum building smoothly, but at five hundred meters, the cabin shuddered and the fuselage groaned. Minh's harness vibrated. As the *Peach* spiraled out of control, overhead safety canisters blasted foam into the cabin. The last thing Minh heard before the foam covered her ears was Kiki's voice.

"They didn't hit us. They didn't—"

Immobilized, blinded, deafened, Minh's biom flooded her with hemostatics, anti-inflammatories, anti-spasmodics. Time stretched. When they crashed, she was mummified in foam, doped up, barely conscious. The concussion reverberated through the *Peach*'s skin. Minh felt it rip through the flesh-and-blood legs she'd left be-hind with her childhood. That flesh knew how it felt when the world tore apart. They remembered what apoc-alypse felt like.

21

IN THE DISTANCE, SHULGI'S soldiers shouted, "A sail! A sail!"

Shulgi squinted upriver. A blue sail with a white circle—his breath left him in a groan. Susa. Her sail, her barge, heavily laden and low in the water. This changed everything. Susa would see his delay in dealing with the monster as hesitation and interpret it as weakness.

He'd waited too long. Time to attack.

~

The *Peach* skidded across the fields, raking through the crops and throwing a plume of dirt high into the air. It tore through a grove of pistachios and almonds. When it hit a rocky outcropping, the fuselage cracked and split, spilling foam. The two pieces spun and flipped, finally coming to rest in a wide drainage ditch.

Minh clawed to consciousness in darkness, entirely swaddled in foam, with messages, feeds, alerts, and alarms all begging for attention. She slapped them all down, kicked hard, and peeled herself out of the foam, landing face-down in mud. A crack of light glimmered, as if in the distance. She crawled to it, grabbed its edges, and forced herself out into the light.

She struggled to focus. Two *Peach*es—amber skips smeared with dirt and bits of plants, landing struts ripped away. No, one *Peach,* but in two pieces—ripped apart as if sawn through by a giant knife. The open sides cupped the earth, edges sunk in sloppy gray mud. Decomposing safety foam floated in the mire.

Overhead, tall palms brushed a bright blue sky. And walking toward her, Shulgi.

"Oh shit, shit, shit, shit, shit, shit," she said.

Sunlight gleamed on his bald scalp, glinted off the camera that dogged him. Shulgi hefted his flail casually, as if weighing it. The leather thongs stretched under the weight of the thorn-flowers. His other fist clenched the hilt of his scythe-like sword. Veins bulged under the thin skin of his forearm.

She grabbed the raw edges of the *Peach* and dragged herself back inside. Alerts and alarms popped into her eye again. She dismissed them—all but Shulgi's camera feed.

The ripped-in-half cabin was packed with decomposing foam. She lashed out with all her limbs, punching through the foam and pulling it off the bulkheads and lights. Her seat was in the way—she wiggled around it. Behind, Fabian was fully encased, bonded to his seat by a thick layer of safety foam. It would hold until he started moving.

If he started moving.

Hamid and Kiki would be in the other half of the *Peach*. She pinged their bioms—Fabian's, too. Green-alive.

Kiki, Hamid, Fabian—are you okay? Answer me.

Hamid's fake popped up and tipped its hat. She slapped it down. No answer from the others. All alive, but unconscious or nearly so. Hurt—how badly? Fabian was safe for now. But Hamid and Kiki—

Shulgi might put his sword through their throats any moment.

Minh pinged the evac gurneys. They were on the move, five minutes away. Then she painted the broken cabin walls with satellite and camera feeds. Shulgi's camera showed him pacing the edge of the ditch, naked, his body flecked and streaked with dirt, eyes narrowed, brow furrowed. His soldiers—their five cameras showed they were running hard. Three minutes away and moving fast.

And Susa. Her barge was six minutes away.

Minh's breath caught; her hands started shaking. She killed the feeds. All that mattered was here and now:

her team, the four gurneys on the way, Shulgi, and the weapons in his hands.

Shulgi was alone. Infrared showed clusters of people all around but staying well back. The only other large organism nearby was Hamid's horse, grazing in the shade of a date palm. No threat there.

She needed to run for the river. Hide and wait for a gurney. Save herself, then rescue the others. It was the right thing to do. The only thing to do.

Maybe, if it were only Fabian. But Hamid. Kiki. Her chest squeezed.

"Shit, shit, shit, shit, shit, shit." Minh beat her fist on Fabian's foam-entombed body. "Where are your health and safety protocols now?"

No answer.

She'd been ignoring her biom for too long; it slid an alert front and center. Mild concussive trauma across the right side of her torso, including bruising to her liver, spleen, and transverse colon. Internal bleeding well under control. Teratomas fine. Spine, lungs, heart, and brain all fine. Her biom was blocking pain and treating her for shock—no wonder she couldn't think clearly. Prognosis ninety percent in forty-eight hours.

Her biom wanted her to lie down and put her feet up. Rest and recuperate.

Hah. It should know her better.

Shulgi wouldn't wait forever, and the soldiers were coming. She had to think of something. Anything.

"I'm the child of your child's child's child." She laughed. It sounded like shattering glass.

Shulgi stepped closer. The babbling was making him curious. She couldn't think, not like this. Short of breath, heart pounding, hands shaking, blood pressure shooting and dropping. If she kept this up, she'd lose consciousness.

Maybe that would be best. She'd already screwed up in every possible way. If she passed out, fate could take its course.

Before another mad laugh could bubble to the surface, Minh dialed herself down. Way down. A chill calm spread from her sternum out to her limbs. She wiped sweat from her forehead and tagged Shulgi with a proximity alarm.

Okay. Think. What assets did she have? Satellites—great. When Shulgi stabbed her, she could replay the last few minutes of her life from a high angle as she bled out into the mud. She had floats, if any survived when the cargo pit split. She had sensors, gauges, cameras, and sampling nests spread over a hundred thousand square kilometers. And she had yottabytes of data funneling from those sensors through the satellites and into the wireframe's information core on the other side of the planet.

She had her legs. They were strong. She could kill Shulgi. Distract him with a camera, get a leg around his throat, and lock down the compression. Now. Before the soldiers arrived. If she got legs around his arms, she might even survive.

Her hands started shaking again. Time travel—that's how to solve this problem. Replay the same scenario over and over, tweaking the decision tree until an acceptable outcome popped out the other end. Wasn't that the whole reason CEERD formed TERN? To save humanity from its mistakes?

Minh finally understood. After eighty-three years, she finally knew the truth. With some mistakes, all you can do is beg fate to deal you a new hand. Lucky, wasn't she, to live so long before being confronted with the consequences of her own stupidity?

Deep breaths. Think. She used to be good at solving problems on the ground. She'd already wasted a whole minute.

First things first: Hamid and Kiki.

She grabbed control of Shulgi's camera and spun it around his head, then pitched it away from the *Peach*. As he twisted to keep it in sight, she slid across the ditch into the other half of the *Peach*.

Not much foam. Just filmy sheets and shreds. Hamid hung sideways in his seat, one arm dangling in the mud. His hair was scarlet with blood.

"No, no, no, no, no, no," she chanted. "Hamid, wake up, wake up. Shit, shit, shit."

His biom was raising a livid life-support goiter on the side of his neck. A deep wound over his eye was crusting over with a thick forced scab.

The safety foam on Hamid's side of the skip had misfired. He'd ridden out the crash unprotected, secured only by his safety harness. The damage could be catastrophic. His brain might be pulp.

She pinged Hamid's fake. *How badly is he hurt?* she demanded.

It grinned. *As far as you know, I'm immortal. I'm going to live forever.*

She slapped it down and turned her attention back to Shulgi. Had he seen her? No, he was distracted, looking the other direction. Now was her opportunity to get the situation under control.

Nothing she could do for Hamid right now.

Kiki, though. Minh wiggled belly-down in the mud and edged around Hamid, clearing the filmy webs with her fingers. Where Kiki's seat should be was—nothing. Minh's gut thudded. The entire floor plate had sheared away. Kiki was gone.

"Kiki, no," she breathed.

"Where are you?" It came out a whine. *Where are you? Where?*

Minh pinged her location. Right there—the satellites said she was in the *Peach*. Except she wasn't. Minh's vision swam. She plunged her legs into the mud, hands, too, digging desperately.

Her hand met a hoof. An ankle, a leg. No, part of a leg. *Kiki.*

Minh clutched Kiki's ankle as though she were drowning. Her breath sobbed. She sent the camera scooting out and around the *Peach,* certain she'd find Kiki's blood and guts smeared across the fuselage.

No blood, none. Kiki was buried in mud, wedged in shadow between skip and ditch. Only her head and part of one arm were visible. Her neck was wrenched around at an unnatural angle and her hand gripped a clump of grass. Her mouth worked as if she were trying to chew through the mud lapping at her chin.

Minh lunged past Hamid. The proximity alarm blared. Shulgi was right outside.

-22-

THE SOLDIERS DROPPED THEIR packs and slid into the ditch. A brief greeting—no time for brotherly effusiveness—then they heaved the egg over. Bits of white foam burst into the air, set into motion by the monster's legs as it fled.

It half-dragged, half-carried two other monsters along with it.

~

Minh grabbed control of every camera in the area and threw them at Shulgi's head. They dodged his skull at the last moment. Safety protocols, accident avoidance. Cameras were not weapons. Minh whined in frustration.

They were still good for distraction, though.

Minh spun the cameras around Shulgi and spiraled them away. He couldn't possibly resist. As far as he knew, this was magic, right? Didn't they believe in magic?

There's your magic, Minh thought. *Go get it.*

Shulgi ignored the cameras. He slid his hand under

the edge of the fuselage and lifted. The *Peach* shuddered. Hamid bounced in his restraints. Minh grabbed at his safety harness, fumbled with the clasps.

The countdown timer on the soldiers flashed zero.

The harness clicked open and Hamid fell into her arms, smearing blood over the front of her coveralls.

Fingers under the edge of the *Peach*. It creaked as it rocked—once, twice, three times.

The *Peach* flipped.

Minh grabbed Kiki and lunged up the bank, clutching Hamid to her chest and dragging Kiki like a rag doll.

Minh. Minh. Minh, Kiki whispered.

Minh couldn't answer—no attention to spare. She sped into a bean patch, smashed through the cane trellises, and ran into a melon field shaded by tall palms and sumac trees. She used the satellite feed to track a route, trying to avoid the datapoints, but people were converging on her location from all over.

Minh didn't even get half a kilometer before the farmers surrounded her, brandishing rakes and hoes. An old woman ran at her, shovel held high.

Minh lashed out two legs and swatted the shovel away. She lost her balance, falling backward, hard, Hamid's limp body collapsing across her chest. She rolled, pushing Hamid toward Kiki.

Grab him, she whispered. *Run.*

Kiki writhed, palms slapping the dirt. Her legs stuttered, beating a tattoo on soil wet with smashed melons. Then she gathered Hamid to her chest and cupped a protective hand over his goiter.

I can't run, Kiki whispered. *My biom is all red.*

Kiki's biom bloomed over Minh's eye. She quickly glanced over the data. Midbrain trauma. Impaired balance, nausea, and confusion. Neuroplastic agents already repairing the damage. Prognosis: ninety percent recovery within a day or two.

If she lived that long.

The old farmer swung her shovel again. Minh yanked it out of her hands. Another farmer swung a hoe. Minh grabbed that, too. Then a rock hit her in the temple. The sky swam with black spots. Alerts blazed across her biom.

"Park!"

One short syllable, uttered with complete authority. The farmers parted to let Shulgi through. The old woman glared up at him, grumbling.

Minh crawled over Hamid and Kiki, tenting their bodies with her legs. Shulgi paced toward her, weapons raised, steps deliberate.

Minh hefted the shovel and hoe.

Play dead, Kiki.

Kiki grabbed one of Minh's toes. *I want to help.*

A piece of melon was stuck to Kiki's cheek. *There's no*

time. Play dead. They won't kill you if they think you're already dead. Minh's eyes prickled but no tears came. *I'm sorry.*

Hamid's fake popped up. *What is this, Minh, your last stand?*

Minh glared at the fake and slapped it down. It popped back up. A wry smile spread over its weathered face.

I always knew you'd go full diva in the end, it said.

She swung the hoe at Shulgi. Weakly. Ineffectually. He avoided the blow with a slight twist of his muscled torso.

Minh was no killer. The only fighting she'd ever done was with her tongue.

She snarled at him. "I hate this shit-ass world of yours. Nothing works the way it should." Her eyes prickled again; her face grew hot. "Not even me, and I don't make mistakes."

If she had attacked him while the farmers were staying back, before the soldiers arrived, she might have knocked him out for long enough to get Hamid and Kiki into the gurneys—maybe Fabian, too. But no chance now. Not one person in the crowd was empty-handed. Even the smallest children held rocks. One young mother picked up a pebble and pushed it into her baby's hand.

Minh swung the shovel at Shulgi.

"I've spent my life avoiding mistakes. But here, I'm a

mess. A joke. Go ahead, kill me. Put me out of my misery."

Shulgi didn't look impressed. He batted the shovel away with the pommel of his sword and spoke. A flow of nonsense syllables.

"Put some clothes on. Aren't you supposed to be king?" Minh said. "What will Susa say when she gets here?"

Shulgi froze. The morning light glanced off his perfect fat baby physique.

"Susa. Susa. Her name gets your attention, does it? Sure, I've met Susa. She has bad taste in friends. You should tell her that."

Shulgi turned away from Minh and looked back at the crash site. Minh glanced at the feeds. Susa and all her attendants were at the *Peach*.

And Fabian was with her.

-23-

SHULGI PURSUED THE THREE monsters through the fields, but only when they came to a stop was he able to get a good look at all of them. The old octopus woman was clearly terrified—of the crowd surrounding her, of Shulgi, of everything. The young woman with goat legs looked strong but was unable to stand; when she tried, she collapsed and retched in the dirt. The third was a small old man, completely human in appearance but diseased and dying. The other two monsters protected him with undeniable tenderness.

A sad trio. He should let the crowd dispatch them. If they were dangerous, valiant monsters, he'd be proud to do battle with all or any one of them. But these were meek, sick, frightened creatures, hardly worth soiling his weapons.

Where was the fourth?

∼

Fabian, tell Susa to help us, Minh whispered. *We're in deep trouble.*

No answer.

We need a minute to get into the gurneys.

A rock hit Minh between the shoulder blades. Pain lanced through her spine. Shulgi barked at the farmer who'd thrown it.

Fabian, why won't you answer?

A small child darted forward, touched Kiki's hoof, and sprang away as if bitten.

Kiki pulled on one of Minh's toes.

I know what to do, she whispered. *I've been looking through the feeds—*

Forget that. Talk to Fabian. He won't answer me.

No use. Fabian's abandoning us. Can't you see the gurneys?

Minh looked toward the sun, shading her eyes. The gurneys were descending over the *Peach,* four stubby gray fingers on a disembodied hand. Above them, a raptor circled on graceful wings.

Minh's heart hammered. She pinged the gurneys. Control block. Health and safety override in progress.

Minh flew a camera in close to Fabian.

What are you doing with the gurneys? she whispered. *Kiki and Hamid are here, with me. We can't come to you. We're surrounded.*

When he looked up at the camera, his expression was stony and pitiless.

You don't get it, do you, Minh? Fabian whispered. *This is the end.*

The end?

Don't worry, though. Calgary won't have to do without you. We are time travelers, after all.

I don't understand.

Let me lay it out for you. I'm salvaging this project. You'll have your data. Not all of it—none of the feeds showing what happened to you. But you'll still be able to write your final report and make our client happy. But it won't be you, not precisely. A different you.

Minh dropped the shovel and the hoe. She sank to the ground beside Hamid. Kiki took her hand.

You'll die here, Fabian continued. *When I get back to TERN, I'll make a quick recall mission, pick up your team from medical, and bring you all forward. Though I'm seriously considering leaving Kiki behind. Even if it would ruin my perfect safety record.*

The gurneys settled slowly on the ground. Their lids slid open. Fabian took Susa's elbow and guided her to the nearest one.

"Look at Susa." Minh pointed and waved four of her legs. "Susa. She's leaving."

Shulgi glanced in the direction she was pointing but couldn't see past the crowd.

"Susa." She scissored two fingers and walked her hand

through the air. "Susa's leaving."

Shulgi barked a command at the guards, and they all turned and ran.

Susa climbed into the gurney. Her attendants screeched, grabbing at her, trying to pull her out. She barked an order and they fell back. She gave another order, and two children ran to Fabian. He boosted them into gurneys, then he leapt into the fourth. The lids hissed shut.

The old farmer retrieved the shovel and hoe Minh had dropped. She scolded the crowd, waving her shovel overhead, as if inciting them to attack.

Kiki shot Minh a bookmark.

Follow my lead.

And then Kiki started to sing.

Minh sped through the bookmark. It was the same feed she'd sent Minh earlier, along with the pottery workshop and the children learning to write. Two people lounging in an alcove. It made no sense. Kiki was concussed. She wasn't thinking properly.

But neither was Minh. And ignoring Kiki hadn't turned out well in the past.

She put the feed in front of her eye and gave it her full attention. The old person was obviously sick, possibly dying. The young one was singing as they held hands. An intimate moment. Loving. Caring.

Kiki lay in the dirt. She held Hamid to her chest, gripping his fingers with one hand and patting his blood-caked hair with the other as she sang.

A slow melody and simple syllables: *lu-lu-lo-shu-sha-glo-to-eh*. Even Minh could follow along. She never sang, but she did now, tuneful as a gas blockage in a sewage pipe. She slid closer to Kiki and took Hamid's other hand between both of hers.

The old farmer lowered her shovel.

You're tough, boss, but I always knew you cared, said Hamid's fake.

The crowd didn't know where to look: The singing monsters, the four gurneys rising into the sky, Susa's howling attendants, or the king standing among them, his face a mask of confusion and dismay.

Minh threaded a leg around Kiki's waist, another around her shoulders, bracing her so she could sit up. She circled Hamid's chest with another and held them both close. She wasn't going to let them go. They were all she had to hang on to.

Minh stroked Kiki's back.

"I think we're stuck here," she said softly.

Kiki wrapped her fingers around one of Minh's toes and squeezed.

The crowd fragmented. Shulgi and his soldiers stood under the rising gurneys, watching them disappear into pinpoints among the clouds. A few people slid into the ditch to examine the *Peach*. Some retreated to the river, to Susa's barge, while others made their way across the fields to the road.

A few people stayed with Minh, Kiki, and Hamid in the melon patch, where the warm morning air was sweet with the fragrance of melon juice. They sat among the buzzing flies, the chirping birds. Their faces were shaded with curiosity and confusion.

One woman, a few meters away, was dressed in pink. She was playing with the laces of her leather wrist cuff and watching Minh closely.

The falconer. Her bird circled overhead.

"We're not going anywhere," Minh said to her. "Nowhere at all."

Minh met the falconer's frank gaze and dipped her head from side to side, like she'd seen on the feed. No idea what it meant, exactly, but did it matter? *I'm here with you. I'm listening. I'm trying to understand.* Something like that.

The falconer dipped her head in return.

Shulgi walked toward them through the knee-high grain, trailed by his soldiers. The wind rustled the stalks. When he got close, the falconer ran to join him. He looked shattered, as if Susa's defection had split his world apart. The falconer murmured a few words; he bent close to listen, and then turned to face Minh.

Minh stayed on the ground. If she died, so be it. She could see the river, and Hamid and Kiki were at her side.

Shulgi leaned down and held out his hand.

Acknowledgments

Lucky Peach would not have existed without the support of many people. First, and always, thanks go to my wife, Alyx Dellamonica, the best person I know. I'm so lucky to share my life with you.

Thanks to Bill, Rhonda, and Kendal Robson, Sue Christie, Sherelyn Tocher, Linda Carson, Caitlin Sweet, Peter Watts, Rebecca Stefoff, Jessica Reisman, Alexandra Renwick, Claude Lalumière, Nicki Hamilton, Denise Garzón, Charlene Challenger, Titus Androgynous, Margo MacDonald, Ming Dinh, Elaine Mari, Jeremy Brett, Dawn Marie Pares, Ryan Abbott, Zane Grant, Usman Malik, Jordan Sharpe, Dominik Parisien, Chris Szego, Madeline Ashby, David Nickle, Kellan Szpara, Keph Senett, Connie Willis, Walter Jon Williams, Sheila Williams, Neil Clarke, Jonathan Strahan, Clarence Young, Anna Tambour, Jeffe Kennedy, and especially Michael Bishop. I appreciate your gifts of encouragement, inspiration, and love.

Thanks to communities physical and virtual: PubQ, ChiSeries Toronto, the SFWA chat room, and Taos Toolbox 2007. Your companionship is no small thing.

Thanks to my wonderful editor, Ellen Datlow, and the lovely people at Tor.com for being with me from end to end.

Thanks to my dad, Bill Robson, long gone. I wish you could read this. I know you'd be proud.

For practical help, thanks to Usman Malik, who kindly fielded medical questions on the fly, and Daniel Potter, whose presentation at the 2016 SFWA Nebulas conference provided me with the teratomas. Neither are responsible for mistakes I've made and science I've stretched.

Finally, thanks to ESSA, the Vancouver environmental consulting company that appears here in entirely fictional form. Your road is high and rocky. I admire you more than you know.

About the Author

Photograph by Maxwell Ander

KELLY ROBSON's fiction has appeared in *Asimov's Science Fiction, Tor.com, Clarkesworld* magazine, and several anthologies. Her *Tor.com* novella *Waters of Versailles* won the Aurora Award, and she has also been a finalist for the Nebula Award, World Fantasy Award, Theodore Sturgeon Award, Sunburst Award, and John W. Campbell Award for Best New Writer. Her stories have been included in numerous year's best anthologies, and she is a regular contributor to the "Another Word" column at *Clarkesworld*.

Kelly grew up in the foothills of the Canadian Rocky Mountains and competed in rodeos as a teenager. From

2008 to 2012, she was the wine columnist for *Chatelaine*, Canada's largest women's magazine. After many years in Vancouver, she and her wife, fellow SF writer A. M. Dellamonica, now live in Toronto.

TOR·COM

Science fiction. Fantasy. The universe.

And related subjects.

*

More than just a publisher's website, *Tor.com*

is a venue for **original fiction, comics,** and

discussion of the entire field of SF and fantasy,

in all media and from all sources. Visit our site

today—and join the conversation yourself.

CPSIA information can be obtained
at www.ICGtesting.com
Printed in the USA
LVHW04s1924080618
580115LV00001B/129/P